ONCE A WIDOW,
TO A
STRANGER

A Contemporary Emotional Romance

MARANDA BALLARD

ISBN 978-1-63814-040-5 (Paperback)
ISBN 978-1-63814-041-2 (Digital)

Unless otherwise noted, all Bible quotes are from NIV.

Covenant Books, Inc.
11661 Hwy 707
Murrells Inlet, SC 29576
www.covenantbooks.com

Thank you to you who chose this book to read.

This book is dedicated to my mother and grandmother, both who dreamed to publish something but was called home to the Lord all too soon.

And to the young, keep dreaming, work toward it, keep your faith, and watch the Lord help you succeed.

As you read this book, please keep in mind, I am not a professional author.

You will find mistakes, and that is okay.

Instead of looking for simple mistakes, grammar, or punctuation, connect with the characters. I write from the heart and the mind.

CHAPTER 1

Mary Ann

Life has not been the same since that tragic night. MaryAnn, once an outgoing person, has grown to be incredibly quiet, does not smile. She knew she had to return to the salon to work, but she was not sure she can return—return to the place. A place where Eli proposed to her just after she cut his hair, the place she found out that she was having her daughter. She was just sitting at her kitchen table sipping what is now a cup of cold black coffee.

"Mom." Deanna, thirteen years old, walked over to the table. "Mom, the bus will be here soon."

"Okay, baby girl. Get your shoes on and grab your backpack."

"Did you pack my lunch today?"

"I did. It's on the counter." MaryAnn looked up into her daughter's eyes.

"Mom, it will be okay, won't it?" Her eyes filled with tears.

"Come here, my precious child. It will be okay. I am sorry. I will try to bring back my smile."

"I miss your smile."

"Me too." MaryAnn embraced Deanna in her arms. "I am going to go to the salon today, maybe not to work but to see how things are going. Maybe tomorrow I will get back up and start doing hair."

"You know, Mom, I miss Daddy too, but I miss you most." Deanna's soft moist blue eyes blinked her sadness away.

That statement hit MaryAnn hard. It has been a month since the accident, a month of hell on earth, depression, anxiety, but yet support. So many neighbors and townspeople have been stopping by, cooking meals, checking on her and Deanna. Jacob has stopped every single day since the day he stepped into the salon breaking the bad news, taking her to the hospital, not leaving her or Deanna's side. How could she pick right back up, when every time she closes her eyes, she sees Jacob, coming into the salon, taking his uniform hat off, holding it in front of him, head tilted down, only to look into her eyes, with his own moistened blue eyes? Then hearing him say the words, "There has been an accident." He has offered to give her the details—details she once asked for—but at that time, he refused to tell her. Maybe, just maybe, if she knew them, it would help her to put some pieces into the puzzle, the puzzle of life. Just maybe.

"Mom." Pulling MaryAnn from her thoughts, Deanna just stared at her mother.

"I am so sorry. I am so sorry." MaryAnn grabbed her daughter and began to sob. "It's not just me that has been hurting since your father died. You have been hurting too. To make matters worse, I have been the most horrible mother through the whole thing."

"No, Mom, you are still the best mom ever, but I am going to miss the bus if you don't let me go." Deanna knew a little bit of laughter could brighten her mother's depression.

"Well, I guess you will miss it. I am never letting you go."

"Mom."

"Okay, okay, silly girl. Go get your lunch. Have a wonderful day at school today."

"I will, and tell everyone in the salon I said hello." Smiling, Deanna grabbed her bag and walked out the door. MaryAnn got up and walked to the door to watch her not so baby, baby girl stand at the end of the driveway. The bus pulled up, Deanna turned around, waved goodbye, and blew her mother a kiss. "I love you, Mom!"

"I love you too, baby girl!" she said while taking a deep breath as she watched the bus pull away. "Well, I guess I should make it to the salon today."

Just as MaryAnn turned around and began to shut the door, a police cruiser pulled into her driveway. Opening the door once again, she stepped outside, as Jacob opened his cruiser door.

"Hey, Mary." In full uniform, standing about five feet, six inches, short crew cut, blue eyes, Jacob walked over to MaryAnn or, as he calls her, Mary. "How are you this morning? Here, I brought you some fresh coffee from Maggy's Place."

"Hey, Jacob, thank you. You know, you do not have to stop every morning, but I do welcome the coffee from Maggy's Place. This stuff is like gold."

"I just want to make sure you are okay. Make sure you do not need anything."

"I am good. I am actually going to head into town this morning, check on the salon."

"That's great!"

"Do you have time? Can you come inside? I want to ask you something."

"Anything for you." Jacob smiled as he followed Mary into the house. He followed her to the kitchen table.

"Jacob, you offered me information that I once asked for, and I am glad you didn't give it to me then, and I know I turned it down when you did offer. I was wondering, is that offer still there?"

"Mary, I told you, whenever you are ready, I will tell you everything. From the time the call came across my walkie till the time I walked into the salon."

"I want to know. I think it will help me, give me piece to a jigsaw puzzle, maybe some kind of closure. Did he suffer? Did he say anything?"

"I will tell you under one condition."

"What is that?"

"That you let me tell you without interruption. I will give you every detail and answer all your questions after I am done."

"Okay."

"Okay." Jacob grabbed her hands. "Do you want me to sugarcoat anything?"

"No. Please, Jacob, I need to know."

"I was doing my normal drive, you know, around town and through the developments, schools. We're getting ready to let out and I like to make sure everything appears safe. The rain just started. It was not too steady yet. The call came across around three. MVC, truck verse rig. I knew right there it was going to be bad. Location was given, and I flew, sirens wailing. I was there in less than three minutes. I was not far from the scene." Jacob was trying to put into terms that Mary would not only hear but understand. Taking a deep breath, he closed his eyes, still holding her hands. "When I turned the corner, I saw Eli's truck. The driver's side was hit by a loaded tractor trailer. I radioed it in. I radioed for the medical chopper to land in the field right next to the scene. I radioed to the hospital to inform them of the scene. I was the first one there. I quickly ran to Eli. He, by the grace of God, was alive, barely able to talk."

*****

"Hey, man, what hurts the most? Can you feel anything?" Jacob's voice filled with emotions as he asked his friend questions. The Black Ford F-250 was mangled, frame bent, the front grill of the semitruck smacked into the front driver's side panel, causing the truck to spin a 180 into the pole.

"All...all...over..." Eli Baker, the head man from the local Ford Dealership, could barely talk.

"I got help on the way, Eli. Hold on. Hang in there, for Deanna and Mary, man. Hang on." Jacob tried to pull on the bent door, but it would not move. Looking up, he saw the fire and EMS's lights. "Help is almost here."

"Jac... Jacob...take...take care of my girls... Tell them, I love them."

"Man, Eli, you're not going to let go, you hear me! Don't you dare die on me, on your family."

"It's...it's peaceful."

"Eli, come one, man, leave that light alone!"

"Promise...promise you take care of them."

"I will, I promise, Eli." Jacob looked over at the fire engine as the first responders jumped out. "Get over here. We are losing him!"

"Officer Shaffer, we got it from here."

Knowing he had a job to do, he let the firefighters do their job to extract Eli from his truck. He walked over to the other set of first responders, tending to the semi's driver.

"Captain, how is the driver?"

"Officer Shaffer, the semi driver had a medical emergency. Apparently, he suffered a heart attack. They are doing compressions on him as we speak. How is the driver of the truck?"

"Not good. It would be a miracle if they pull him out alive. Did you get any identification on the semi driver?"

"Yes, we pulled his wallet from his back pocket. He is not from around here. My best guess: he was picking a fresh load from the warehouse. Here is his emergency contact. As soon as they extract the pickup driver, we can get you his wallet to contact his family."

"No need, it's Eli Baker."

"No!" Captain Tash grew up with Eli. He quickly ran over to the truck. "Lieutenant, how much longer till you get him out?"

"Not much longer now, Cap. Maybe thirty seconds."

"Tammy, get that other stretcher over here, now. The medical chopper should be landing soon. Eli is to go up in that."

Jacob and Captain Tash just stood, frozen, watching as the crew removed the driver's side door. Eli was still pinned; they had to put airbags in to widen the bent dashboard away from his legs.

"We have no pulse!" Tammy yelled. "Get him on the back board."

The lieutenant carefully pulled Eli from the wreck, sliding him onto the back board. Tammy quickly started the chest compressions.

"One, two, three, four, five... One, two, three, four, five..."

Sandra the paramedic pulled up to the scene. Taking notice to all that was happening, she sent John the second paramedic over to the semi driver as she grabbed her AED.

"How long has he been down?"

"A few minutes. We had to extract him from the truck, took about three or five minutes. We lost pulse about two minutes ago."

Sandra hooked up the AED in between compressions.

"Stand clear."

Everyone watched the machine analyze. Silence. What only took a few seconds felt like forever. Jacob stood there, in pure shock.

"Asystole." Sandra looked up. "He is gone." She talked into her walkie. "Car 2, paramedic 1, go to main."

"Go for main."

"Main, I need to do a DOA. Male driver, time of death: fifteen twenty-eight."

"Confirmed, DOA of one male driver, fifteen twenty-eight."

"I am so sorry, Officer Shaffer, there is nothing we can do for him." Sandra covered Eli over with the white blanket.

Jacob lowered his head into his hands. He felt someone's hands on his shoulder. He turned to see Captain Mark Shell standing next to him.

"I heard the DOA call over the radio. This is one that is hard to swallow. Is it true? Is it Eli?"

"Yes."

"How is the other driver?"

"Critical. He is taking what should be Eli's ride to the hospital, in the chopper."

"His wife."

"I will inform her. I do not know how, but I promised him I would look after them, so I will inform her. What about Deanna? I am sure he was on his way to pick her up from school."

"I will go get her. I already have the school delaying the dismal because of the accident. They will be taking his body to the hospital, so I will meet you there with her."

"Okay."

"You should head over. The talks among this town travel fast. I have some of the patrol officers taking care of traffic."

"What am I going to say to her, Mark?"

"Just be honest with her. She will know something is wrong the moment you step foot in the salon. Women can sense it."

"He was my friend, my friend since we were in diapers."

"I know." Captain Shell patted Jacob on the shoulder before embracing him into a hug. "You are his friend first, but now you must be the sergeant and inform the family."

Taking a deep breath, Jacob gathered his emotions. He watched them load the body of Eli Baker into the ambulance. All the first responders stood, lowered their helmets, their hats, as the wagon drove off, lights on, siren silenced. Jacob watched until it turned the corner and was out of sight, then with his head lowered, he headed for his cruiser. How was he going to tell Mary that her best friend, the love of her life, the father of her daughter, her husband, life partner, better half, was now her angel? How was he going to break the news? Sliding into the cruiser, he put it into gear, driving away from the mangled truck.

"Promise to take care of my girls" replayed over and over in his head. "It's peaceful." Was Eli in comfort and not suffering? Without realizing, Jacob pulled up to the salon. He slowly put it into park, getting out, holding back as much as he could from letting the tears fall. Opening the front door, he was greeted by Natalie.

"Hey there, Officer Shaffer, what can I get you this afternoon?"

"Is Mary with a client?"

"No, she is in the back. Is something wrong?"

"Take me to her please."

"Okay. Jacob, what is wrong?"

"Natalie, I need to speak with Mary before anyone else."

Natalie sensed the urgency and walked Jacob to the back office, where Mary was sitting, going over bills and paperwork.

"Jacob, what a surprise visit." Mary looked up. "Jacob, what's going?"

"Mary, there has been an accident, a bad accident."

"What? Is Deanna okay?"

"Yes, she is fine. It is Eli. He was on his way to her school. A loaded semitruck, the driver suffered a heart attack, ran a red light, hit the front panel of Eli's truck, spinning him, sending him into a pole. He was alive when I got to him."

"WAS?"

"He made me promise to look after you and Deanna. He said he loved you two so much. He said he was at peace. He died at fifteen twenty-eight...three twenty-eight. Paramedic Sandra hooked him up to the AED. There was no pulse, no rhythm. Captain Shell is picking Deanna

up from school, so she does not see the scene, and will be meeting us at the hospital where they are taking his body."

"NO, NO, this cannot be happening. Tell me this is not true, Jacob. PLEASE TELL ME THIS IS NOT TRUE!"

"Mary, I wish I could." He caught her as she collapsed into his arms, sobbing, hyperventilating. "NATALIE, we need a cool towel and water please."

"MARYANN!" Natalie exclaimed. She quickly ran to the sink, soaked the towel, grabbed a bottle of water from the snack table, and made her way back to the office. "Jacob, what happened?"

"She fainted."

"Why?"

"I just told her that her husband was just killed in a car wreck." Still holding Mary in his arms, he sat her down into her chair then placed the towel on the back of her neck. "Come on, Mary, come on. Wake up."

Slowly she came to.

"Jacob, please tell me it's not true."

"Mary, I wish I could. Come on, let me take you to the hospital. Deanna will need her mother. She is going to be so confused as to why the police captain is taking her to the hospital."

MaryAnn went to stand and could not. Her legs wobbled then gave out on her. Jacob quickly scooped her into his arms. She wrapped her arms around his neck and buried her face into his shoulders, the tears flowing as a water goes over the waterfall. Everyone froze in the salon as they watched them walk to the front.

"Natalie, take care of the salon. Make some calls and cancel her appointments for the next week or so."

"I have it all under control. Let me know if there is anything you need or MaryAnn needs."

"I will." Jacob walked out the door, with Mary in his arms. He opened the passenger's side of the cruiser and lowered her into it. He was not going to make her ride in the back. Shutting the door, he walked to the driver's side, sliding in, turning the engine over. Looking over at MaryAnn, he grabbed her hand.

"Mary, it will be okay, you will be okay."

She stared out the window, like she was staring into space. Tears streamed down her face without a sound coming from her lips. Jacob squeezed her hand as he headed toward the hospital—no sirens, no lights, no words. The ten-minute drive to the hospital was in silence, the longest silence ever. As they approached the light just before the hospital, they could see all the fire trucks, the ambulance, and several police cars.

"Are they all here for Eli?"

"Your husband made a huge impact on this town and now everyone wants to give back by supporting you and Deanna."

"I never realized the impact he made," MaryAnn whispered. "I will never understand why. Why was it his time? We were working on our marriage, fixing it."

"I know, but even though this past year your marriage was not perfect, you were fixing it. I want you to know, Mary, you and Deanna were his world. He loved you two so much."

"Thank you, Jacob." *Taking a deep breath, Mary released her hand from his and wiped the tears from her face.* "I guess we have to go in. Will they have him cleaned up? Will Deanna and I be able to go and say goodbye?"

"Yes. They will put him into a room and not the morgue."

"Will you stay with me? Stay with us?"

"Of course." *Putting the gear into park, turning the cruiser off, Jacob took one big deep breath.* "Ready?"

"Will I ever be ready?"

"No, but remember this: it is not goodbye, but I will see you later on the other side. Come on." *Jacob opened his door, getting out; everyone's eyes turned to his cruiser. He walked around the front of the cruiser to the passenger's side. Opening it, he held his hand out to Mary's.*

Looking up, she placed her hand into his. Slowly stepping out, she tried so hard to hold back the tears until she saw her: Deanna, standing at the top of the steps. MaryAnn lost it. Deanna came running down the steps, past all the first responders standing there.

"Mom!" *Deanna yelled.*

MaryAnn could not explain anything to her. Sobbing, she wrapped her arms around Deanna. She placed a kiss on top of her head as she held her super tight, tears flowing. Everyone stood there watching, watching

MaryAnn hold onto her daughter, the daughter that is yet to be told her father has died.

"Why are you crying?"

"Come on Mary, Deanna. Let us go in the hospital to talk." Jacob placed his hand on Mary's shoulder as they walked toward the hospital. Up the steps, he grabbed the door, held it open as they walked through it. Looking around, he saw a conference room door open. "Over there, Mary."

"Okay. Come, Deanna, we need to tell you something."

"Okay." Deanna followed Jacob, as her mother continued to hold onto her, into the dark empty room. She watched Jacob move out two chairs so they could sit.

"Jacob, I can't." Crying uncontrollably at this point, Mary continued to hold on to Deanna.

"I have it." Sitting into the chair on the other side of Deanna, he turned to her. "I need you to understand something. You are loved so much by so many. You are the most matured smart thirteen-year-old I have ever met. Some would say you have a mind of a young adult. What I have to tell you, though, nobody, especially your age, should have to be told. There was a reason why your school delayed being let out. There is a reason why Captain Shell brought you here. There is a reason why Mommy is upset and why I am here. Your father was involved in an unbelievably bad accident. I was the first on the scene of the crash. I talked to him before he died. He told me he loves you very much." Jacob could not fight the tears back any longer. "He made me promise him to look after you. I asked him to not let go, I asked him to stay, but his injuries, you have to understand, he said he was at peace."

"My...my...dad...my dad is dead?" Deanna's eyes looked up into his, wide, full of shock. "He died?"

"Yes."

"Baby girl, we are here to see him, if you want to."

"If you don't want to, I can wait in the hall with you. Let Mommy go in."

"Will he be full of blood?"

"No, they will have him cleaned up," MaryAnn whispered.

"I don't think I want to see him."

"That is fine. If you change your mind, we can go in." Jacob wiped his face with his hand.

"I don't think Mommy should go in alone. Can I stand in the hall by myself?"

"How about I get Captain Shell stand with you?"

"I would prefer if someone was standing with you, baby girl." Mary found her voice. She was surprised how well her daughter was taking the loss at the moment.

"Okay." Her eyes glazed over with moisture.

Standing from the table, Jacob walked out the room, leaving Deanna and MaryAnn alone.

"Are you okay, baby girl?"

"He is really gone?"

"Yes, he is really gone."

"I don't know how to feel. I am sad..."

"Do you feel like it's not real?"

"Yes."

"That is why we are here, seeing him, saying words that we know he cannot hear, but saying them helps us."

"Words?"

"Telling him how much you love him, how much you will miss him, saying goodbye."

"Oh. Making it real."

"Yes."

"Mommy, why did he have to die?"

"I don't know, baby girl, I don't know." She took a deep breath. "I do know, Daddy would not want us to be sad for a long time. It's okay to be sad for a little bit, but I think Daddy would want us to live life, to find our happiness once again." Tears continued to flow down as MaryAnn tried to be the strong mother that she needs to be.

Jacob returned to the room with Captain Shell.

"Hey, Deanna, MaryAnn." Captain Shell walked over to them. "They have him in the next room over when you're ready."

"I am ready." MaryAnn stood up, holding Deanna's hand. "Mark, thank you for standing out in the hall with Deanna. If she changes her mind, you can let her into the room."

"You're welcome." Captain Mark Shell, a man that seldom is speechless, has no words.

Jacob held onto MaryAnn's hand as he guided her to the room. Looking over at Deanna, who stayed right next to Captain Shell, MaryAnn slowly opened the door. Walking into the room, there on a gurney, under a white blanket, Eli laid. Turning her head into Jacob's shoulder, he held her.

"Take your time," he said in whispered tones. Jacob pushed his tears back. Looking at the nurse who was standing next to Eli, he motioned for her to remove the blanket from Eli's head.

"Eli," MaryAnn whispered. "Eli, it wasn't your time. Our time should not abruptly end. What about Deanna. Eli?" MaryAnn stood looking at his face. "I will forever love you." She turned her head back into Jacob's shoulders. He held her tight. Looking at the nurse, he motioned for her to cover his face.

"Come on, Mary."

"Where do I go from here?"

"One day at a time. One moment at a time."

"I should not be a widow at thirty-nine."

CHAPTER 2

Jacob

Jacob sat there as he listened to Mary sob. He knew she needed to hear the words; he knew she needed to know what exactly happened.

"Thank you. Thank you for telling me."

"Mary, you're welcome." What else was he supposed to say?

"I just don't know how life is going to be. I know, one day at a time, but so much easier said than done. Do you know what Deanna said to me today, that really hit me hard?"

"What did she say?"

"That she misses her daddy but misses me most."

"Oh, Mary, I don't know what to say to that. She is a smart thirteen-year-old. A little wise for her age."

"Jacob, I don't know how to fix me."

"Mary, you're not broken completely. Just your heart and that will heal. Trust me."

"How do you know, Jacob, how?"

"I suffered a broken heart a long time ago."

"What happened?"

"It wasn't death related, so really, I should not be comparing it to your situation."

"But it still broke your heart, and a broken heart in any form sucks, so tell me please."

"I fell in love with a girl and never told her. She ended up in a marriage with another man. I should have told her."

"Where did you meet her?"

"Well, we actually met in high school. She was a freshman and I was a senior, but she didn't know me from the man on the moon then. I ran into her years later at her job."

*****

The bell rang, first day of Jacob's last school year. Officially a senior and then it is off to the police academy, following his dreams. Opening the front double doors, there seemed to be a lot more freshman this year then there has been in the past. For a small town, there were a lot of people and a lot of kids. Walking past the freshman hall, of course the normal stares of fright from the freshman class. Just as he turned the corner to head up the steps, a book fumbled out of the hand of her. Her, the one who looked into his blue eyes deeply with her sparkling deep-blue eyes, taking his breath away for a split second. Bending down, Jacob grabbed her book.

"I am so sorry." She stood there with shaking hands and lowered her head. Her voice was soft and sweet.

"It's okay. High school can be terrifying yet awesome. You will be okay."

"Thank you."

"You're welcome. See ya around." Jacob walked away. "See ya around?" he whispered to himself. "You fool, you didn't find out her name or give her your name."

"You know, talking to yourself, people are going to start talking about you." Eli came up from behind, pushing Jacob's shoulder a little.

"Ugh, Eli."

"Dude, what has your panties up in a bunch?"

"Do you always have to be such a jerk?"

"Shit?" Eli cut Jacob off. "Well. You're like talking to yourself, and being all sensitive, dude, you should be owning the halls right now. It's our senior year, man."

"This freshman girl, she dropped her book in front of me."

"Oh my, sound the alarms! Lock all the doors. We have a tragedy here: a freshman stopped a senior!" Eli started shouting, joking around.

"*Whatever, man.*" *Jacob started to become annoyed.*

"*Dude, this is serious. You're getting all pissy. You never get like this.*" *Eli shook his head.*

"*You know, Eli, just because you're a senior and eighteen does not mean your language has to be all crappy.*"

"*Whatever, dude. Just tell me what has you all tangled up.*"

Jacob just shook his head.

"*I picked her book up, like a gentleman that I am and you're not.*"

"*Ouch, dude, I will let that punch slide. Go on.*"

Jacob just rolled his eyes and continued, "*Well, she, um, she caught me off guard. She kind of took my breath away with these amazing blue eyes. Her voice was soft, sweet, gentle, like an angel.*"

"*Did you get some digits?*"

"*No, man! I am so mad at myself, kicking myself. I did not even tell her my name or get her name! I just said 'see ya.'*"

"*Wait, hold up!*" *Stopping outside of their homeroom, Eli stared at Jacob.* "*You're telling me, for the first time ever, some girl has made your world flip with just a look and a simple word and you didn't even get her name at least? Like are you for real?*"

"*I know! Eli, I know! It was like instant connection and all she said was 'I am sorry.'*"

"*Dude, we are going to find this girl! You will get her number, take her out, and finally get laid.*"

"*Sex is not everything, you know.*"

"*Yeah, well, that's because you haven't had some.*"

"*Call me old-fashioned, but I want to wait. I have a lot going on right now.*"

"*Dude, no, that is how your Bible-loving family raised you.*"

"*I don't even know how I became friends with you some days.*"

"*Yeah, well, we are, as girls calls it, best friends.*"

"*Well, I am proud of my family and my morals. Maybe you should gain some before it's too late.*"

"*HA!*"

"*Let us go into homeroom. I need to sink in a hole and it's only the first day of school.*"

The last bell rang as they stepped inside. Jacob just kept to himself. Throughout the day, as he walked to his classes, all he could think about were her. He looked for her as he walked through the halls, only to be disappointed when he did not see her. Lunchtime came. Jacob met up with Eli and headed to the cafeteria; he was sure to see her then. Freshman ate just before seniors. Sure enough, there she was. He noticed her right away.

"Oh, is that her?" Eli noticed Jacob's eyes frozen on one girl. "Let's go over to her."

"No, no, Eli, not right now. She doesn't need me hounding on her, not on her first day."

"Jacob, come on, man."

"Eli, if you dare go over to her, I will never forgive you."

They watched her as she walked toward the door they were walking in. She looked up, smiled as she noticed Jacob, sending his heart racing.

"Hi," she was softly speaking as they met at the door.

"Hi." Jacob's heart skipped a few beats. "Hope your first day is going smooth."

"It is."

Eli just stood there in shock. His well-built friend was acting like a puppy with his tail between his legs.

"I am happy to hear."

"Hi, I am Eli by the way, and this guy here that you have met twice now, who forgot to tell you his name, is Jacob."

"Seriously, Eli, go have a seat." Jacob shot Eli a glare of death.

"Nice to meet you both, but I need to hurry to my class." She looked into his eyes yet again before turning and hurrying to her next class.

"And again, you did not get her name. What the hell am I going to do with you, Jacob!"

"Whatever. Whatever, man." Jacob walked over to the table and sat down, shaking his head. Jacob sat in silence, looking out the window. The summer has not been easy for him: losing his grandmother, the person that raised him, helping his grandfather figure things out. Things just were not great, and now this. Eli being Eli is pushing Jacob to the edge.

"She said hello, you said hello, but what you didn't do next is just stupid, man." Eli shoved a piece of pizza rolls into his mouth. "The next

word should have been, 'My name is Jacob. What is yours?' Nooo, you had to ask her how her damn day was."

"Enough, Eli, ENOUGH," Jacob growled through his teeth. "Look, right now, my goal is to get through this year, get through the police academy, and make sure my grandfather is okay. Unlike you, I do not have the time to goof off, screw whatever comes my way. I must be an adult."

"Sorry, Jacob." Eli took a sip of his water. "Why do you want to be an officer anyway? As kids, you always wanted to be a lawyer or doctor."

"Why not? It was an officer that saved me. Why not give back and do it in return?"

"Got ya. You're right."

"What about you? Growing up you wanted to play football for life. Now you're not even playing for high school."

"I will eventually take over my dad's car dealership."

"I guess we both are going different ways."

"Yeah, I guess."

The rest of the day, Jacob could only think of her. Who was she, why hasn't he seen her around town? She cannot be new; she had friends with her. Before he knew it, the last bell of the day rang. He gathered his books and headed for the hall, looking for her; he wanted to know her name, who she was. No such luck. It was not until he stepped outside that he found her, sitting on her bus. He put his head down as he headed for his truck. Tomorrow is another day, to find her, talk to her some more. He figured he would arrive a little earlier at the school; that would give him more time with her. That is the plan. Nothing can change that plan. Starting his truck up, he wanted to pull out before he got stuck behind all the school buses. Turning out of the parking lot, he headed down the road, only to be detoured, an accident up ahead. Seeing Sergeant Mark Shell, he rolled his window down.

"Hey, Serg. What is going on?"

"Oh, hey there, Jacob. We have a fatal MVC, double fatalities. It is a mess. Captain and the detectives are there now trying to figure things out as they pull the bodies. I came down here, I just… I knew them. Very nice folks, quiet, kept to themselves. It's a shame, you just never know when your life path will be suddenly changed and you're called home."

"Who was it?"

"Now you know I can't tell you until I inform their daughter and rest of the family."

"That is a shame. They had kids. How many cars involved?"

"Three, theirs, a mustang, and a semitruck. It is not pretty. From what I can gather, the mustang is the cause of it all. That driver has been airlifted. The driver to the truck is okay but a mess mentally."

"Sorry to hear. I will have Grandpop and I sit down and pray over them."

"That would be a good idea. Now get home before he worries."

"Stay safe."

"You know it, boy."

Jacob drove away, with the accident on his mind, with the girl, with all that has happened. He replayed the scene after his grandmother's funeral in his mind.

"Jacob, I can't understand. With all the sorrow and wrongdoing, you have such a strong faith that this is how it's supposed to be. Your parents overdosing when you were a little child, you are seeing them lying there, gone. Your grandmother who raised you dies of a sudden heart attack. Your grandfather is in despair. Here you are, leaning on your faith. I just don't understand."

"Eli, it's not for you to understand until you're ready to understand it. The only way I can tell you is this: without pain there would be no sorrow in life. Without sorrow there would be no compassion. Without compassion, how do we love, care for others?"

Jacob took a deep breath, wondering who were called home in such a tragic way. What was the mustang driver thinking? Sometimes people make the wrong choices in life and others have to pay greatly for it. Just like he made the wrong choice and did not get her name. Determined, Jacob made up his mind to get her name, to ask to carry her books to homeroom, to be the gentleman that he is.

Tossing and turning that night, Jacob could not get the car accident scene from his head and the daughter, whose life was just shattered. Back to the mystery girl.

The sun finally peaked through his window shades. Springing from his bed, Jacob quickly threw his pants on, a shirt, grabbed his bag and keys, running down the steps.

"Why are you such in a hurry this morning, Jake?"

"Hey, Grandfather, no reason. Just want to get a good parking spot in the school parking lot. Have they mentioned the names yet for the accident?"

"Nope, not yet. From what I have gathered, though, the driver of the mustang is in critical condition. They are not sure if he is going to pull through. That was young Tommy from on the other side of the town, you know, like twenty-four or so."

"Really, he has a younger sister and brother?"

"Yes, they say he tried to pass the truck on a double yellow and the semi was coming. He swerved back into the lane but only to clip the bed of the truck. Those poor people didn't see it coming nor did they feel a thing."

"You never know when your time is up. I just feel really bad for their daughter. To have your world flipped in a matter of minutes."

"Sad, very sad. Well, make sure you drive safe to school."

"I will."

"Love ya, boy."

"Love you too, Gramps." Jacob chuckled a little at their inside nicknames.

With a few steps, he opened his door, started his engine. It did not take him long to get to the school, living only a few blocks away. The buses had just begun to pull in. Parking his truck, he sat there waiting for her bus. He remembered she was sitting on bus 42. His nerves started, and the butterflies began to flutter; it was crazy how this one girl he just met made him feel this way. Her bus pulled up. He got out of his truck and stood against the wall by the door. He was not going to miss her getting of the bus. The door swung open. Student after student stepped down. The last one stepped off, and the doors closed. The bus pulled off. She was not on the bus. Shaking his head, Jacob was certain she was on bus 42.

"Look at you, Mr. GQ, leaning against the wall. Are you stalking a certain girl?"

"Eli, you know, you can be such a jerk"

"Ass. I know you want to say it, church boy, and yes, I am an ass."

"Again, why are we friends?"

"Because you have no other choice." Eli chuckled. *"So where is she?"*

"I don't know. She never got off the bus."

"It's the second day of school. Is she skipping already? My kind of girl!" Eli clapped his hands. Jacob shot him a look. "Let's just go inside. Maybe she got a ride to school."

"Maybe." Jacob had a knot in his gut, a bad feeling. They walked in the door. Several freshmen were standing by her locker, whispering with sorrow face. "What the heck is going on?"

"Dude, how am I supposed to know? Why don't you ask them?"

"Ha, nah, I am not going to pry. It is not my business."

"You know, man, you're such a wimp. I will ask."

"Eli, don't. It's not our business." It was too late; he had already walked over to the group.

"Excuse me, what is going on?"

A young girl looked up at Eli with shock that a senior was asking her a question. Staring blankly, Eli asked again.

"Yes, I am Eli, a senior, asking you all, freshman, what is with the tears and sorrow?"

"Well, if you genuinely care, in which you don't, one of the freshman girls just lost both her parents yesterday in an accident. We all grew up with her and her family. She is being transferred to the next town over and living with her grandparents."

"Ah shit, I'm sorry, that sucks. Was this her locker?"

"Yes. What does it matter to you?" The girl snipped at Eli.

"It matters to my boy over there. He kind of bumped into her yesterday a few times and this time was going to ask for her name and walk her to class, that's what it matters. No need to be a little ignorant." Watching his choice of words, Eli turned around and walked back to Jacob.

"What did they say?"

"Dude, let's step outside."

"No, man, what did they say?"

"Your mystery woman, she is being transferred to a town over, living with her grandparents."

"Why?" Jacob did not know why he needed to ask; he knew why.

"Her parents, they were killed in an accident last night."

He did not know her, he did not know her parents, but his heart just shattered into a million pieces. His eyes, they filled up. He put his head, trying to not show his emotions.

"Excuse me, I just want to tell you, you made her day yesterday, with your kindness." A young girl came up. "Jacob, right?"

"Yes. If you talk to her again, please let her know she is in my prayers."

"I will. Have a good day."

The girl walked back to her group.

"Dude, can you get the assignments today? I just want to go home."

"Yeah, man, why didn't you ask that girl for mystery girl's name and maybe number to reach out to her?"

"What's the point? She does not need me hounding her. She is going through something nobody ever should go through."

"Jake, you went through it. At least reach out and give her support."

"I saw the accident. I saw it on my way home yesterday." Taking a deep breath, he continued, "I would be just a memory to her, a good one from the day her life was shattered. Just get my work today. I am going home."

Eli watched Jacob leave.

*****

Jacob was looking up into Mary's eyes, wondering if she will make the connections, that she is the mystery girl. It took just a few minutes and the light went off. Her eyes flooded with tears.

"Jacob, you described my parent's accident. You described my first and last day in my first freshman high school. You described the sweetest guy I met."

"I am him."

"Why didn't you tell me?"

"By time I realized it, you were already engaged to Eli. You were already in love with him, the fool that didn't realize who you actually were."

"Still, why didn't you say something? I tried to find you after my parents' funeral, but you had already left."

"Like I said, you and Eli were both head over heels in love by time I put two and two together. There is a code among brothers, and I was not about to break it."

"Are you still…do you still feel the same way?"

"Your husband just died the exact same way your parents died. My best friend, I held him when he took his last breath. I am not going to answer that question."

"Damn it, Jacob, tell me! Why haven't any of your other relationships lasted? You had what, three? Very nice women. Jacob, TELL ME."

Standing up, walking over to MaryAnn, he bent down, looking into her eyes.

"What do you think?" He pulled away and headed to the door.

"Jacob, please don't leave without telling me. Did I pick the wrong guy?"

"Mary, you have always been in my heart, my mind. My heart shattered the day my best friend introduced me to you, knowing I have seen your eyes before, and then when he asked you to marry him and you told your story about your parents, I knew you were my mystery girl. My heart shattered. Eli knew too, at that point, who you were, and he apologized, but he loved you and you loved him, and there was nothing I could do. So yes, Mary, it was you who broke my heart a few times. It was you whom it belonged to. Nobody could be you, why nobody worked out, but you are my best friend's widow. You chose him, and there is nothing we can do to change that."

Jacob put his head down and walked out the door, leaving MaryAnn speechless. She stood blankly for a moment or two before jumping up, running to the door.

"JACOB."

It was too late; his cruiser had already pulled away. Things were now even more messed up. Her husband is dead, her best friend, his best friend, turned out to be that mysterious senior that made her heart pulsate. How did she miss the signs? How did she not recognize Jacob right away? Her memory from before her parents' death was a fog. That night she came home to an empty house. She was looking forward to telling her mom about her first day, her first day ever in school. Being homeschooled for the first eight years, her parents were so nervous about putting her into high school, but it was something she truly wanted and begged for. She wanted to tell them about the mystery tall handsome senior who helped her, who asked how her day was. But nobody was there. The lights were out.

CHAPTER 3

Mary Ann

Walking into the kitchen, MaryAnn looked around to see if her parents left a note. Her mom's car was in the driveway, but her father's truck was gone. There was a knock on the front door. Walking to the door, opening it, standing there were three officers.

"Can I help you?" Nervous tones slipped through her lips.

"Are you MaryAnn Dunn, daughter of a Mr. Marshal and Mrs. Dakota Dunn?"

"Yes, they are my parents."

"May we come in?" The officer took off his hat.

"Yes. What is this all about? Are my parents okay?" Taking a deep breath, MaryAnn moved aside, allowing the officers to come in.

"We hate to inform you, there has been a tragic accident."

"Wait, what?" She was losing all the air in her lungs.

"Your parents, they did not make it." As much training as the officers have, nothing prepared them for the silent cries of a young fifteen-year-old made.

She stood there staring at them, unable to breath. Did she hear them right? Her parents were dead? How could that be? This could not be happening. What in the world? This must be a sick cruel prank. It just must be. Tears streamed down her cheeks, yet not a single sound has escaped, nothing but soft air moving past her lips.

"*MaryAnn, do you have anyone we can call?*" the officer finally spoke. "*MaryAnn?*" Nothing; she was unresponsive, in pure shock. "*Call for an ambulance.*"

"*No, no, no need to put her through all that.*" Sergeant Shell walked in the door. "*Give the girl a moment. She will come to. You call the ambulance and they will put her on the psych ward or call child services, none of which she needs.*"

Sergeant Shell walked over to MaryAnn. Standing in front of her, he took his arms and wrapped them around her, exactly what she needed. She went numb and fell into his arms, sobbing out loud.

"*Shhh, my dear child, shhh.*" He looked at the other officer. "*Right there, by the phone, an old-fashioned personal phone book. Look for a number under Mom or something, maybe something is in there.*"

"*My grandmother and grandfather Dunn, my father's parents, are whom I have left,*" MaryAnn finally whispered. "*That is all I have left.*"

"*Okay, MaryAnn. Is it under a name?*"

"*No, Mommy always called them Ma and Pa. She would have it as Ma, Pa Dunn.*"

"*Do you want to call them? Or should I have the officer call them?*"

"*My parents, they talked about you. Did you know them?*"

"*Yes, your father and I, he helped me with some things around my home. Your mom would send over the best baked goods I have ever tasted. I always told your father she should have her own bakery.*"

"*Can…can…*" MaryAnn could not get her words out.

"*You want me to call them?*" Mark understood between her sobs. She nodded her head yes. "*Okay. Here, sit here on the couch. Where is your kitchen?*"

MaryAnn pointed past the hall.

"*Go get her a glass of water please,*" he ordered the officer. "*The rest of you may return back to the station. The station chaplain is still there and waiting in case any of you need to talk to him.*"

Picking up the book, he skimmed to the letters M after he saw nothing in the D section. Top section, just as she stated, would be Ma, Pa Dunn. He picked the phone off the receiver, punching number after number, hearing the ring, taking a deep breath. One life has already been turned upside down; now he must give the worst news to a mother and father over the phone.

"Hello, Dakota, how was Mary's first day of school?" a soft gentle voice answered the phone.

"Hello, Ma'am, this is Sergeant Mark Shell. Who am I speaking to?"

"This is Dorothy Dunn. Is everything okay?"

"No, ma'am. I think you and your husband should drive to your son's home so we can talk."

"Sir, what is going on? You are scaring me. Did something happen to my granddaughter?"

"No, ma'am. She is okay."

"Did something happen to Marshal or Dakota?"

"I would much rather talk to you in person."

"Don't tell me, was that them, on the news, the accident? Tell me that was not their truck. Tell me, please."

"Mrs. Dunn, I think it's best to talk face-to-face."

"Please, I beg of you, please."

"Yes, ma'am. That was them."

"Oh NO!" Dorothy yelled out. "MaryAnn. Was she with them?"

"No, ma'am. She was at school at the time and the buses were routed completely away from the scene."

"What is going on?" a male's voice was heard in the background. "Who is that on the phone, Dot?"

"Sergeant Shell, he is at Marshal's house. That accident we saw on the news, the one with the truck." Dorothy put her phone on speaker. "Sergeant, you are on speaker. My husband, Andrew, is here. Please, just tell me what is going on."

"Yes, that accident was in fact Dakota and Marshal. They…" He looked over at MaryAnn, who was staring off into space. "They were killed on direct impact. MaryAnn is sitting here, in complete shock and needs her grandparents."

"My sweet girl." Dorothy did not have time to sit and think how she just lost her son; her concerns were on her granddaughter. "Can you stay there with her until we are able to make it there? We are an hour and half away."

"Yes, ma'am. I can stay as long as you need me to."

"Thank you, Sergeant Shell. Tell her we are on our way." Dorothy hung the phone up, looking over at her husband, Andrew, who stood there, frozen.

"My boy. That was my boy?"

"Andrew, please, we don't have time to collapse. We have a young teenager who needs us know. Our granddaughter just had the rug pulled right out from her feet. She needs us more than our sorrow needs us."

"Dot. How the heck are you——"

"Andrew, it is not our job to question why things are the way they are or why things happen. We just must trust this is the path that it is supposed to be. MaryAnn, her life was spared because they did not listen to us. They put her into the school. Had they listened to us, she would have been with them. We would have lost her too."

Dorothy walked over to her husband and placed her hands on his face, looking into his eyes. The man just lost his only boy; she just lost her only son. It would hit them when the dust settles, but she cannot let it hit them now.

"Andrew, I can only pray that we can get through this right now. Your granddaughter, our granddaughter, needs us, more than ever. She needs us to be strong. I need you to be strong."

"Why are you taking this better than I am?" Andrew's eyes swelled. "Dot, that is my boy."

"Andy, I am only strong because I have to be and you being stronger will allow me to breathe, to do what I have to do for our granddaughter. You are my rock. I know this is all a shock, I know this hurts so much for you. It does me too. He may have been your boy, your right-hand man, your best friend, but he was my son. She was the daughter I never had. But, Andy, we cannot dwell on their death. We have business to do first. There will come a day we both will break, but that day is not today."

The tears dropped from his eyes, one eye at a time. She softly wiped them away. Death is not always easy to handle, especially when it is your own child, but when a child is left in the wake, you have to find the strength to push through your pain and heartache.

"Andy, let's go."

Sergeant Shell looked out the door. The sky began to open; the rain started to fall. The thunder echoed in the distance. He could not shake the scene of the accident out of his mind. They had no idea what hit them. Turning to look, MaryAnn was no longer in the living room.

"MaryAnn?"

No response.

"MaryAnn?"

Again, no response.

"MaryAnn?" Growing worried, he started to walk toward the hallway. "MaryAnn, are you okay?"

No sounds.

"MaryAnn?" Panic filled his lungs. Turning the corner, she caught his eye.

There sitting on a bed, holding a pillow and shirt, MaryAnn was staring off into space. She glanced up at him as he walked into the door.

"This was their room. These were their things. My mom could not sleep without her pillow and my father loved this shirt. He would wear it on Sundays after church when we would go out to dinner. Mark, will he be able to wear this when we have his funeral? Would we be able to do an open casket?"

"We can arrange for this shirt to be put on him."

"What about open casket?"

"You know, MaryAnn, those details, I rather not discuss."

Her eyes grew wide, understanding just how bad the accident was. "Did they suffer?"

"I do not even think they knew what hit them. I don't know if it will help, but when the first responders checked on them, they found they were holding hands."

"They loved each other so much. They were each other's best friend. They both were my best friend." Taking a deep breath, she looked down, squeezing the pillow tighter. "I lost my parents. I lost my best friends. What in the world am I going to do?"

"You know what you are going to do, MaryAnn. You're going to cry." He sat next to her, wrapping his arm around her. "You are going to cry a lot, but as the days come and go, you will learn to breathe. You will learn to find yourself again. Figure out who you are, who you will

be, what you will do. But in the meantime, give yourself time to cry, to grieve. Even though you will be an hour and half away, always remember you have a friend here, me. My phone is always on if you need anything. Your parents, they are the sweetest people I have ever met and did not deserve this. So promise me, if you need me, you will call me."

"I promise."

"Promise me that you will allow yourself to cry, a lot, for a while, but then allow yourself to heal too."

"Okay."

"Promise me you won't lose your faith in all this. You need your faith. It will help you with your second promise."

"It's hard. I keep asking myself why it was their time and in such a way. It was not my time to lose them."

"We can't ask why. If you do, you will be let down, for it is not in our place to ask why and we will never get that answer. He has a plan, and it may not be the plan we want. He has one. When you are feeling weak, remember Philippians 4:13: 'I can do all this through him who gives me strength.' Look to him for your strength."

"Okay." MaryAnn knew he was right, but it was so much harder to do. "You know, Mark, I could have been there with them. I could have been in the middle of the truck bench where I normally sit, in between the two of them."

"But you weren't. Your life was spared for a purpose."

"Just as I thought today was going to be the best day in my life. I was coming home from my very first day of school, let alone high school. My mom homeschooled me. I wanted to tell her how awesome my classes where, and how very welcoming the school was, especially this one boy. He is a senior, truly kind to me. My first impression of my first day in an overwhelming large high school was a great impression because he took the care and concern to make sure I was okay in the hall and asked how my day was going as we passed through the cafeteria doors. I wanted to tell my mom the teachers were awesome, leave out the boy part with my dad because he was so overprotected. I wanted to tell them I was looking into a few afterschool clubs to join. I wanted them to come with me to the first football game."

Squeezing the pillow tighter, MaryAnn burst into tears. Sergeant Shell squeezed her tighter. What else could he do?

"Why don't we go sit on the front porch and watch the storm come in? Sitting on your parents' bed will only make it worse for you."

"Okay."

Standing up, he reached his hand out, taking her hand, helping her to stand. Still clutching on to her father shirt and mother's pillow, she followed behind him as they walked to the front of the house, the thunder clashing, lightning striking, rain falling. Sergeant Shell opened the front door, stepping out onto the large front covered porch.

"It looks dry. Do you want to sit out here or in the living room?"

"No, I like it out here." MaryAnn walked to the chair with the biggest cushions. She slid down, sitting as she brought her knees up to her chest.

"Your grandparents will be here soon. They seem like they will take great care of you."

"And homeschool me." The disappointment slipped through her lips.

"Maybe not. You can ask them to send you to the local high school there."

"I know they won't. They fought with mom and dad about keeping me from going to the high school here. They do not like the public-school system. To them I am not getting the best education that I would get with the homeschool program."

"Why are they so against public schools?"

"God is not in it."

"So why not send you to a Christian school?"

"Their words: why should we pay for a school, when we can teach it on our own home?"

"Yeah, that is a tough argument to beat."

"Yeah, it is, isn't it?" MaryAnn chuckled a little. "Well, when I have children, they can have a choice. I can homeschool them if they wish or they can attend public schools."

"That sounds fair enough to me." Sergeant Shell kept MaryAnn talking; keeping her mind off her parents' death is his main goal.

Sitting there, silence fell as they listened to the pit-a-pat of the rain hitting the cars, the crash sound as lighting struck in the distance and the roar of the thunder. A soothing sound. MaryAnn sat there, staring off. Moments later, she broke the silence as she softly started to sing..."Amazing Grace."

MaryAnn stared out into the stormy sky. Verse by verse, word by word, she sang her mother's favorite song, forgetting she was not the only one there. The tears dropped as she continued to sing from a whispered tone to a full-blown emotional solo. Neighbors who stayed in their home as they watched through their curtains as the police brought the news to her stepped out onto their porches to listen—listen to the young girl sing her broken heart out. Just as she sang the last verse, she started the first verse with more emotion.

"A...mazing grace, how sweet thy sound. That saved a wench like meeee. I onceee was lost, but now I am found, wasss blind...but...now... I see." She wiped her tears away, blinking her eyes. MaryAnn noticed she was no longer alone. She did not hear her grandparents pull up; she did not hear the neighbors walk over and stand in front of her porch as the rain stopped. Everyone stood there in awe, tears falling down their cheeks.

"Mary." Dot walked up onto the porch and wrapped her arms around her.

"Nan." She took a deep breath. "I didn't hear you pull up."

"My dear child, when did you learn to sing like that?"

"It was my mom's favorite song. I just wanted to sing to her. I forgot I was outside."

*****

Sitting at her kitchen table, MaryAnn placed her hands over her face as her tears fell. She knew she had to fix this. She needed to be the mother her daughter deserves. The mother she once had, the mother that her nan was once to her, the mother she knows she can be. She needs to fix her friendship. She cannot lose him again. There was always something so special about Jacob, and she could never figure out what it was until now. It makes all sense. The day Eli introduced her to him, the smile that beamed across his face and the look in his eyes, look of happiness yet sorrow.

*****

"MaryAnn, I want you to meet my best friend, Jacob." Eli stood tall, proud. Never in his mind did he think the beautiful young girl who walked into his car dealership looking to buy a new car would walk out with a man as part of the package.

"Hello." She looked into Jacob's eyes. They looked familiar.

Her soft voice, he has heard it before, but where? Where has he seen those beautiful blue eyes before. Jacob lost his voice. Something so familiar with Eli's new girlfriend has him stomped. Has he pulled her over? Racing his memory, he thought of every woman he has come across.

"Hi," he said, finally finding his voice. "Nice to meet you."

Reading the confusion on Jacob's face, Eli spoke up.

"Yeah, man. She walked into the dealership and I sold her on the whole package, a car and me. What a steal."

"Man, I don't even know how you won her over with your romance." Jacob was still trying to search his memory. "MaryAnn, are you from around here?"

"Once upon a time. I moved to the next town over my freshman year of high school. I went here for like one day and something changed my course." MaryAnn did not want to into details of her tragic past.

A lightbulb went off in his head. His eyes grew wide. She is the girl. THE GIRL, and Eli has her. Talk about a hit to the gut. Eli saw Jacob's face grow pale.

"Well, it was nice to meet you. Eli, I have to go." Quickly turning around, Jacob just about ran to his truck.

"Jacob!" Eli yelled, but Jacob did not respond. "I wonder what got to him."

"Do you think he didn't like me?"

"MaryAnn, please, you are the most likeable person I have ever met."

"Just odd when I mentioned about school, his face was like something hit him and he went pale."

"I know, it was odd. I will give him a…" It hit Eli. The mystery girl from high school was only there for the first day and disappeared. Jacob's heart was stolen and broken all in twenty-four hours' time. "So you said you went to the local school."

"Yes, I was homeschooled up till the first day of high school. And well, something happened, and I had to move. I pretty much blocked that day out of my mind. I was again homeschooled after that."

"It was bad, that something."

"I really don't want to talk about it, Eli. We have only been dating for a month."

"I understand. One day, promise to open up to me please."

"I will." MaryAnn kissed him on the cheek. "I need to get going. I have class. Almost done with this course and one more and I should be on my way to my own salon."

"I know you can do it." He returned the kiss. Eli watched MaryAnn walk away and climb into her SUV. As she pulled away, he grabbed his phone and called Jacob.

"Hello," Jacob answered.

"Jacob, you sound like you just lost you puppy."

"What can I do for you?"

"Tell me it's not her. Tell me that the girl I eventually want to marry, tell me it's not your mystery girl."

"It is." Jacob shook his head. "You have her now. She is head over heels for you and you seem to be head over heels for her."

"Damn, Jacob. I do not know what to say, man. If I had realized who she was when I first met her, you know I would have walked away."

"I know. I know."

"What do you want me to do? You know our friendship means more than a girl."

"Answer me this. How do you feel about her?"

"I am crazy over her. She is the most amazing person I have ever met. She makes me want to be a better me."

"Well, I can't stop that. If you're happy, man, you want to marry her, something I never thought I would hear come from your mouth, then you do it. Just take care of her. I know it's crazy, it was so long ago, and it was one day, but dang."

"I know, man, I know." Eli ran his hands through his hair. "Will you be okay?"

"Yup. Just take care of her. Give her the world."

"Should we tell her?"

"No, Eli. We should just keep this between us. It was not meant to be. She found you."

"Well, in her defense, my job invited the public to come look at my cars to buy, yours the public cringe when those lights show up behind their cars."

"Eli, Eli, Eli." Jacob chuckled. *"Going to let that slide just a little."*

"Truth will set you free, my friend." Eli regretted just as he said it.

"I know you meant that as a joke, but given the state of my mind right now, it went to her. Telling her would be wrong. She didn't know I fell head over heels for her and doesn't need to know."

"I know, man. Between us." Eli knew his friendship with Jacob was more like brotherhood. *"Hey, when the time comes, will you be okay to stand up as my best man?"*

"Dude, you know it! I would be so honored." Jacob tried to put excitement to his voice, but he knew Eli was not buying it.

"Okay. Man, I will let you go. Talk to you later." Eli hung up the phone. He knew Jacob was not okay at the moment, but later on he can only hope he will be.

*****

How did she miss the signs? MaryAnn kept trying to wrap her mind around it. She knew she had to talk to someone and the only person she could trust was her best friend, Natalie. Natalie was taking care of the salon in her absence. Picking the phone up, she dialed the salon number.

"Good morning. Thank you for calling Beauty is in the Hair. Jennifer speaking."

"Hey, Jenn. Is Natalie there?"

"Hey, MaryAnn. It is so nice to hear your voice. We truly miss you here."

"Thanks, Jenn."

"Yeah, Natalie is here. She is just finishing up a client."

"Can you tell her to call me when she has a moment?"

"She is about done if you want to wait a second."

"Sure. How is the salon doing?"

"We are okay. Your clients do come in, but they are worried about you. We just tell them you will be back soon."

"You can start to book me on Tuesday through Thursday, full day."

"Really?" Jennifer, the youngest of the stylist, started to jump up and down. "That is so exciting. Can we put that on our web page, too, that you are returning?"

"Yes, please do. Eli would be so disappointed that I have not returned yet."

"He would have understood." Jennifer was Eli's cousin.

"Thank you, Jenn. I needed to hear that." MaryAnn took a deep breath. "Book me easy for the first week, okay? Extra time in between chemicals."

"Deal. I will make a note for whoever takes the calls."

"How is the new girl, Stephanie, working out?"

"Um, well…"

"I can tell by your tone, you're not too fond of her."

"No, she is totally a negative person, not nice to the stylists but puts on a face for the clients."

"I have heard that. I will handle that when I return."

"Okay."

"Thanks, Jenn, for working as hard as you have, stepping up and taking extra hours. I really appreciate it."

"That is what family is for." Jenn took a deep breath. She knew MaryAnn did not have much a family. "Here is Natalie."

"Hey, girl. I see you're returning."

"Hey, Nat. Yeah, I need to get out of my slump. I need to get back into reality."

"Well, I am very excited to have you return. Does Deanna know?"

"I will tell her when she gets home from school. Do you have time if I come in to fix my hair up?"

"Do I have time? For you, of course."

"No, seriously, I do not want to take you from your clients."

"Yes. I have the rest of the day open."

"Okay, let me get dressed. I will send Deanna a text just in case I am not home when she gets done school."

"Okay, I will see you soon."

MaryAnn put her phone on the table. Pushing herself up, she walked to her room, the room she once shared with Eli. Even though they were struggling at the moment, she loved him. Taking a deep breath, she stepped in the room for the first time since they laid him to rest. Since then she has been sleeping in their guest room. Brushing back her tears, she went straight for her closet, grabbing jeans and a shirt.

"I need to clean his stuff out. Repaint this room, making new. Maybe that will help me to move on." Whispering to herself, MaryAnn got changed and grabbed her keys. "I got this. Death has not brought me down in the past. It will not bring me down now."

Slipping her shoes on, she walked out the front door, texting Deanna on her way out.

"Deanna, I love you. You are my rock. I am sorry. I am working on getting me back. I am heading to the salon. Natalie is going to fix my hair up. Maybe change it, cut it off or something. When I come home, can you help me? I think I want to get Daddy's stuff out of the bedroom. Is it too soon to do that? We can donate it to the shelter. He would appreciate that knowing his things would keep someone else warm. Let me know when you get out of class. Love, Mom."

Opening her car door, she slid into the driver's seat. Starting the engine, taking a deep breath, she backed out of the driveway. She decided to take the long way, avoiding the road where the accident occurred. Only problem with that, she would pass her house—the house she once shared with her parents. It broke her heart to see it there, abandoned. It has been twenty-four years since her parents' death, ten years since her grandparents joined them. The house has sat vacant for the twenty-four years. Her grandparents kept the upkeep on it, paying the bills, making sure all was well with it. They could not let it go. It was the one thing they could hold on to other than MaryAnn. When they died, MaryAnn did not know what to do, not knowing they kept it all this time until their will was ready. She could not bring herself to go inside the house. Everything was left right where it was the day the accident happened. Jacob patrols it; he has always checked on it, even when her grandparents were alive. Did he know it was her house?

She was driving down the road, road of memories, road of the day that changed her life drastically. She slowed down to look at the house. Locked up. The grass was maintained by the one neighbor. One day she needs to thank him. Flowers still laid on the gate. So many years later, people still leave flowers and letters on the gate. Seeing the police cruiser turning onto the road, she started to drive away. Last thing she needed was to see Jacob. One day, she will ask him if he knows the story behind the house he watches. Driving past the officer, she looked over, and sure enough, it was Jacob. His eyes were shocked as he noticed her driving by. She has to fix this with him.

Ten minutes later, pulling up to the salon, her phone began to buzz with a text alert.

"Mom, I am glad you getting your hair done. Tell everyone hello. Who will get me off the bus?"

Dang, MaryAnn is so used to having Eli being able to get her off the bus. With his parents in another state, she had only one option and that was Jacob. Here goes nothing. She dialed his cell-phone number.

"Are you okay, Mary?"

"Hey, Jacob. I am fine. Can I ask a favor of you please?"

"Yes, anything."

"I decided to drive to the salon. I am getting my hair done. I need something to pick me up and get ready to return. I am not sure if I am going to make it to get Deanna off the bus, and it's too late in the day to change her bus routine."

"I don't mind. I will patrol over that way and grab her. Normal time?"

"Yes, thank you so much."

"Do you want me to bring her to you? Or stick at the house?"

"No, you can bring her to me. I owe her a date night."

"She would love that."

"Oh, I know." A little giggle was let out. "Hey, Jacob, we are going to have to talk about today, sooner than later."

"I know."

"When we do, I want you to tell me why you patrol that old abandoned house."

"That was out of the blue. I can just tell you now." Taken aback, Jacob continued to talk before she could respond. "Ever since I joined the station, Captain Shell has made it known to each officer, sergeant, whoever was on the force, that we were to patrol that house, make sure nobody trespassed. In the beginning the owners used to come out once a week to mow, make sure everything was okay, but they passed away ten or so years ago. So the captain makes sure the taxes are paid, and the neighbor now once a week mows. We often offer to pay for his service, but he said his family would forever be in debt to original owners of the house, whatever that meant."

"Younger or older neighbor?"

"The son. Why are you asking?"

"Jacob, sometimes the Lord puts people in your path to help you through some really difficult times, and sometimes it just takes a moment for you to see them all."

"Mary, are you sure you're okay?'

"Better than okay, I am fine. Thanks for grabbing her." MaryAnn hung the phone up. Pieces of her puzzle were falling into place. Getting out of the car, she walked into the salon, where everyone froze.

"MaryAnn." Natalie walked over and gave her a big hug. "Oh my, look at your hair."

"Hey. Hi, everyone. First, I want to thank each and every one of you for your well wishes. I am here, I am returning, some things will be changing," she said, glancing over at Stephanie. "Some things, not so much. I still need your patience. You know as much as I do, the first two weeks or month of hearing 'How are you doing?' 'How are you hanging?' 'I am so sorry to hear about Eli' will most likely have my emotions on a rocky roller coaster, but that is okay and is expected. So keep the stock of tissues in the back and we will be a-okay."

"It's good to have you back." Jennifer walked up, giving her a hug.

"Thanks, Jenn. So, Nat, I want it cut off. I want the works. No pixie, but something fun, something new. Something totally up to you. Turn me from the mirror and surprise me at the end. Stay away from platinum blonde and black is my only request on the colors."

"Yes! Girl, let's do it. I have been waiting so long to chop all this off!"

"Ha! I know you have been. Just do it. Use my station though please. We need to talk."

"Oh, serious?"

"Yeah, why I want to be in the back? Plus clients cannot see me unless they come get their hair washed. I need a me moment."

"Yes, yes, you do." Natalie smiled. "Hey, listen up, everyone. She is not here. I am not here. We have business to discuss and hair to do. Jennifer, you manage the front register and phones for me please. Stephanie, you can do the afternoon cleanup round."

"What? Isn't that Jenn's job?" Stephanie spoke up with pure negative attitude. As soon as MaryAnn heard that, she walked up to her.

"Stephanie, you listen to me and you listen hard. I gave you a chance to work here, a chance no other salon or barber would give you because of your piss-poor attitude. In this salon we work as a team and treat one another as if you are family. There is no room for negativity here, no room for 'Isn't that her job' teenage drama crap. You're how old? Act it! AND NO, it is not her job. It is everyone's job to keep this salon clean. Trust me, even though I was sitting home in shock and grieving the loss of my husband, clients told me what was going on in this shop, the good, the bad, and the ugly, and you by fact is the ugly. They told me the things you were saying. So I will say this once and only once. Push one more button and you will be out the door. You will be damn lucky if you can find another job of any kind in this small town. Do I make myself clear?"

"Yes."

"You might want to find yourself in church and talk to God. You need him in your life." MaryAnn was looking over to see Maggy, an older client, sitting in Jennifer's chair. "Maggy, I apologize. That was something that was not meant for a client to hear."

"Mary, don't you worry about me. I agree with everything you just said. She needs Jesus in her life for sure. I am glad to see your spunk is back along with you."

MaryAnn walked over to her station. Cards laid on top. She picked them up and placed them into her purse, knowing if she opened them now, she would not be able to control her tears.

"So now you got that off your chest, what is on your mind, Mary?"

"Natalie, you remember me telling you the story about the mystery man in high school?"

"Yeah, the man that in one breath swept you off your feet, the one man that if you found him could steal you from Eli."

"Yeah, him."

"Yeah, what about him?"

"I found him."

"WHAT?"

"Let me just say, he found me, a long time ago. He has been in my life for a very long time. He just come clean about it, and I just don't know what to do."

"Wait, is it who I think it is? If so, how did you not realize it?"

"I blocked everything out from that horrible day. Only thing I can remember is knowing he stole my heart, and I didn't know his name or what he looked like because I blocked it out."

"So who is it?"

"Jacob."

CHAPTER 4

Jacob

Jacob ended the call. He was glad she called. The way he ended his last visit with her, now knowing they were each other's mystery person. Jacob needed to talk to someone. Turning the cruiser around, he headed back to the station. The only one he could talk to, who knew him well, and that was still alive was Captain Shell.

"Hey, Cap. Got a minute?"

"Hey, Jacob. Yeah, come in."

Jacob took a deep breath and shut the door.

"More than a minute, and serious." Looking up, Mark put his pen down. "What's going on, Jacob?"

"A lot. First, I have to get Deanna off the bus for Mary. Mary is getting her hair done in the salon and is not sure how long she is going to be. I figured I would patrol over that way around that time."

"Just take a half day. I am actually overstaffed today."

"That works."

"Now tell me what is really bothering you."

"Mary. Mary is my mystery high school girl," Jacob just blurted it out.

"Okay."

"And I do not know what to do about it."

"Does she know?"

"Yes. I told her today. It kind of slipped out. We were talking about the accident. She wanted the details and I gave them to her.

Then she asked me why I never settled down, how I had opportunities with a few nice girls."

"But they were never her."

"Right." Jacob looked up at Mark. "Did you know?"

"I figured it out, the way you always helped Eli out, always overdoing things for them both. Simply the way you looked at her. Did Eli know?"

"Yes. I told him the day he introduced me to her when I figured it out."

"Yet you still let him have her."

"She didn't know. He was head over heels for her, and it was years prior for one day. So I let him fall in love and be happy. She loved him."

"Now that she knows, what does she have to say?"

"I don't know. I walked out of the house."

"So within what, an hour or so, you told her how her husband died, his last words, then told her that you are her mystery man and she was your mystery girl from high school, that she married the wrong man and you did not give her time to respond."

"For what point? She is the widow to my best friend, my brother. It's not like we dated in high school. We just said hi and a few more words."

"Need I remind you Proverbs 16:4? 'The Lord works out everything, and a season for every activity under the heavens.'"

"I am not understanding."

"My boy, he put her in your path in the beginning for a reason."

"But why not keep her in my path? Why take her away and send her down Eli's path?"

"There is a greater picture that you are not understanding. You were her happiness on a day she lost her parents in a wreck. The wreck you drove up to that day when I told you I could not tell you who they were until I told their daughter. You were her smile that day, but at that time you could have been her reminder of that day too. She had to go on to a different path, to learn how to cope, how to handle her emotions and her memory. She couldn't remember what you looked like, but she remembered how you made her feel safe when she was scared in the school, and that feeling is what she held on to. That afternoon when she sang her mother's favorite hymn."

"So I would have reminded her the day her life was just flipped right upside down."

"Something like that."

"What about now?"

"Now, you have been in her life, you have been there for her and Eli for so long that you no longer would remind her of the worst day of her life. You would remind her of the best days yet to come."

"I don't know, Mark."

"I do." Taking a deep breath, Mark sighed. "Fix this. You both deserve a happy ever after but be the friend first. She needs her friend more than anything right now."

"I know," he said, rubbing his hand through his hair. "I just do not know how to fix it."

"Pick up Deanna. Step one. She called you. She is still talking to you. Fixing it will be no problem. Let her bring it up to you."

"When she called me, she asked me the strangest question, just after I saw her parked outside that house you have us all watch."

"What did she ask?" Mark never told Jacob the details about the house, who the original owners were, how that was MaryAnn's house.

"Why do we take care of it?"

"She didn't tell you why she was parked in front of it?"

"No, and it is not the first time I have seen her parked there."

"Well, you ask her. It is her story to tell, not mine."

"So you know?"

"I do." Mark closed his eyes.

*****

"Thank you, Sergeant Shell, for staying with our granddaughter," Dorothy whispered as she held MaryAnn tight.

"No need to thank me. Dakota and Marshall were great people. They have done a lot for not just me but this whole town. They will be greatly missed." Mark held the door as they walked into the house.

"This house." Dorothy looked over at her husband. "We can't let this house go ever. One day, Mary will want to visit it. If we let it go, she will not have the option to close this chapter in her life."

"I understand." Mark lowered his head. "I will have the police force keep an eye on it."

"You know you do not have to do that," Andrew spoke up with his scratchy deep voice.

"Mr. Dunn, you're right. I do not have to do that, but I want to. Your son, he was one who would drop everything to run to help someone in need. He was one to help someone struggling. Your daughter-in-law, well, let me just say, the homeless will miss her greatly. They will miss all her baked goods she would take down to the shelter or hand-deliver. We may be a small town, but we have our fair share of people down on their luck. The Dunns never judged anyone, always looking at the positive in someone, anyone they crossed paths with. They did it without the spotlight as well. Every time we were to give them a community award, they would decline it. The Dunns are the humblest people I have ever had the pleasure to meet, and our community will forever be in debt to them. So, sir, it would be an honor to watch after their home."

"It's Andrew." He reached his hand out, shaking Mark's hand. "Thank you for the kind words. I suppose a few extra sets of eyes will help keep this place safe."

"Then it is a done deal."

*****

Shaking his head, pulling back from his memories, he looked over at Jacob.

"It is her story to tell, my boy. Now go be her friend. Go be the person she turns to. Go pick Deanna up and not in the cruiser either."

"You are right. I need to be there for her." Jacob stood up. "So take the rest of the day off?"

"Well, it's really not the rest of the day. You have what, an hour or two before you have to get Deanna. Why don't you go home, get changed, take a moment for yourself to breathe? You never take a day off for yourself."

"I usually don't need an extra day off for myself."

"Well, we all need to once in a while."

"Okay, Cap. I will take a few hours to myself. I will do one more check on that house and head home."

"Sounds good. See you in the morning."

Jacob walked out the office, went to the front desk, informing them he is off shift. Strolling out the front door, he got in his cruiser and left the station. Driving toward the house, this time he will do door checks. Seeing how curious Mary was about the house has Jacob wondering why. Why has she sat outside the house in his car numerous times? *Why was she asking about our reasons of patrolling it?* Jacob pulled up the driveway.

"Hey, Serg."

"Hey, Miles. How are things around here?" Miles was the neighbor who took care of the yard.

"Quiet as usual."

"That's a good thing. I am just going to do a door and window check and be heading out. You still have my cellphone in case anything should happen?"

"Yes, sir."

Jacob shook his hand and walked to the house. First, he walked around. Everything was still locked up and in order. Captain Shell does a weekly inside check, makes sure the pipes are okay, keeping the condition of the house ready as if someone would to move in that very day. He continued to walk around. Windows still closed. Nothing looked out of place. His phone started to ring.

"Hello?"

"Jacob, are you still at the house?"

"Hey, Cap. Yeah, heading to check the front door."

"Can you do an inside check, flush the toilet, run the water in the kitchen? Make sure everything is good to go. I am not going to make it this week."

"I don't have a key."

"Yes, actually you do. My house key that I gave you is actually the key to that house."

"Really? Okay. Not even going to ask why you had me believe all these years. I had a key to your house when it is the house we are watching."

"Technically this is my house. I pay the taxes and electric bill on it."

"Good point. Still do not understand the reason behind all that, but okay. Anything else I need to do inside?"

"Your questions will be answered sooner than you know it. No. I have to come out next week with my wife to do the monthly cleaning. Just make sure the temp is no lower than sixty-two and no higher than sixty-nine."

"Okay." Jacob hung the phone up, still confused by Mark's answers. *The answers to my questions will come sooner than later*, he thought. Walking over to the front of the house, reaching into his pocket, he pulled his keys out. Sure enough, the key fit. Slowly opening the door, creaking just slightly, he walked into the living room. As he turned the lights on, he saw it.

Sitting on the mantel was a big photo of Mary. The Mary he saw in high school. Next to that photo was a family photo of her parents and her, sitting on the log by the river. His hand guided over the mantel. The house, it was just as it was left the day of the accident. He walked over to the phone where he saw the phone book lying open. Ma and Pa Dunn. He walked to the kitchen, turned the faucet on. Water poured out, warm. Looking over, dishes still sat in the strainer, untouched. The kitchen table still had the mail sitting on it from that day. Taking a deep breath, he walked to the back of the house to flush the toilet. Seeing the happy family photos along the hall, photos of Mary and her mother, Mary, and her father, just her parents, all smiling and laughing. Tears started to fill Jacob's eyes. He found the bathroom, flushed the toilet, only to let the tears flow as he noticed the toothbrushes sitting there untouched.

"This is Mary's house," he whispered to himself. "No wonder she stops here."

"You're correct."

The voice startled Jacob as he drew his gun.

"Cap, don't you know not to walk up behind someone?" Jacob eased his gun back into the holster. "What are you doing here?"

"When you said you were going to stop by to do a door check, I waited a few minutes and then followed you out. You need to know. This may be her story to tell, but maybe by knowing you would understand not to push the subject, like I know you would have done."

"The house is left untouched."

"That is correct. That day her grandparents met me here, I was sitting with her the whole time. They picked her up, packed a few items, and she has not been back since. She sits in her car, unable to come in. Her grandparents wanted her to have the option to return."

"The beds are left unmade."

"I made a promise to not move a thing. When my wife and I come in to clean, we simply vacuum and dust without moving anything. Run the water, check the pipes. Oil the hinges."

"When I saw her photo on the mantle, it hit my stomach, but seeing everything as it was left...the photos, the dishes, the toothbrushes..."

"It's heartbreaking."

"Yes."

"Now, does it make more sense she needs her friend more than anything right now?"

"Yes."

"You are put in life where you are needed. God knew one day he would need you to be there for her again. That time is now."

Jacob wiped his tears away.

"You cannot let her know, you know. Let her tell you. Let her invite you into a place in her life that she has blocked out."

"So much easier said than done."

"You're telling me. Look at how long I have been holding this secret from you, from everyone but my wife."

"Why have you?"

"You weren't there to see her in pure shock, to see her in dismay of the death of her parents, to hear her sing with so much emotion, 'Amazing Grace.' I have no choice but to pretend not to know."

"Won't she be upset that you knew the whole time and didn't say a thing?"

"I honestly do not think she will. A piece of me thinks she remembers, she knows."

They walked out to the front door.

"I won't say anything." Jacob walked down the steps as Mark locked the door.

"Everything okay over there?" Miles walked over. He has been so curious about the story behind the house, the house his father told him to watch, to mow.

"Yes. We were just checking to make sure all the plumbing was okay. You know over time how that could become an issue," Mark spoke up.

"Just never seen two officers go inside, had me worried."

"No, no. Everything is fine. I just want Jacob to know what to do in case I ever go on this vacation my wife has been begging for."

"Sir, question."

"Yes."

"Should I be concerned that a car with a lady in it, she stops and stares at the house for, sometimes, fifteen minutes? It has been happening a lot more lately."

"No, she is no threat."

"Okay."

"Miles, thank you for all your help. I greatly appreciate it, and I promise one day your questions will be answered. You just have to let the good Lord continue with his Book of Life until that chapter is unfolded."

"Yes, sir. You are very welcome."

Miles walked back to his yard, Jacob got in his cruiser and left, and Mark just looked back at the house. He can see the young Mary sitting there, singing, before turning to leave.

Jacob noticed the time and quickly ran into his home, got changed, grabbed his truck keys, and ran out the door. Mary's house was not too far from his, but he did not want to be late for the bus. Pulling up into her driveway, just in time. The bus pulled up just five minutes later.

Noticing Jacob, Deanna ran off the bus and gave him a big hug. "Hey, Jacob."

"Hey, Dee girl. How was school?" He waved to the driver as she pulled off.

"School was good. I got an A on my test."

"What! An A! Do you know what that means?"

"What?"

"A trip to the ice cream shop before we go to the salon."

"REALLY?"

"Uh, yeah! Let's go inside so you can put your things away." Jacob walked to the door, unlocking it.

"I want to bring my book bag, I have homework to do, and Mommy might be longer than she said."

"That is fine. Just put your gym bag away."

"Okay." Deanna ran to her room, throwing her bag on her bed. "Hey, Jacob."

"Yeah."

"Is Mommy going to be okay?"

"Oh, my sweet girl, she will. Mommy just went through so much in life that sometimes, she has to hit a rest button to grasp things. I think with her going to the salon today is a positive step. A step in the right direction to being okay. We just have to be here for her."

"I might have been mean to her this morning. I want her to know I love her, I miss Daddy so much, but I miss her being her most. She is alive."

"Sometimes I forget you're only thirteen. You act and talk like you're so much older. Your mom knows you miss your dad. You were not mean to her. You actually helped her. Your words pushed Mommy out of this house. Your words opened her eyes."

"So I helped Mommy?"

"Yes, you did." Jacob smiled; he could not help but notice just how much Deanna looked like the little girl in the photos on the wall at the mystery house, how much she looked just like her mother. "Come on, my girl, let's get some much-needed and rewarded ice cream. I think I am going to have chocolate chip mint with rainbow sprinkles and whipped cream."

"Hey, that's what I was going to pick!"

"No way! That's my favorite."

"It's mine and Mommy's too!"

"How awesome is that!"

Jacob closed and locked the door behind them. Walking to the truck, he sent Mary a text message.

"Take your time. I got Deanna, stopping for some ice cream first, then we will be there."

"Thank you, Jacob. I owe you big time. Thank you for being the most amazing person, friend. Let me treat you to dinner. Tomorrow night?"

"I would like that."

Jacob smiled. They are going to be okay. Life will be okay. Pulling out of the driveway, he headed for town. There was only one ice cream shop to go to, owned by Stacy, Mark's wife.

"Hey, Jacob." Deanna looked over. "Do you know what my mom is doing to her hair?"

"No clue. She just said she needed a change."

"She texted me earlier asking to help get my dad's clothes to donate."

"Did she?"

"Yep."

"I think your mom has to close a few chapters in her book of life in order to move on. And I think the way your father died, it opened an old chapter that was not fully closed."

"You're talking about her parents."

"Yes. She was so young when she lost them, and now your father."

"I am glad she has you to talk to."

"You have me too, if you ever just want to talk or get some ice cream."

"Really?"

"Yep. So you ready for that ice cream because we are here!" Jacob put his truck into park. Deanna's eyes lit up as her face brightened up.

"Well, let's go." She jumped out of the truck.

Chuckling, Jacob shook his head and got out of the truck. Shutting his door, he walked to the main door to the ice cream parlor. Grabbing it, he opened it for Deanna, allowing her to walk in first.

"Well, hey there, Jacob and Deanna. What a nice little surprise!" Stacy shouted from behind the counter.

"Hey, Stacy. Yeah, I figured I would treat Deanna to some ice cream before I took her over to her mom at the salon. Mary is getting a makeover."

"Oh, how nice. So, Miss Deanna, what would you like?"

"We are going to actually have the same thing," Deanna spoke softly.

"Oh really?"

"Yes." Jacob smiled. "Go ahead, Dee. You can order for the both of us."

"Okay. What size?"

"Small is fine."

"Okay. Two small chocolate chip mint with a little bit of hot fudge and whipped cream and rainbow jimmies."

"Easiest order yet." Stacy smiled. "Go ahead and have a seat. I will bring them to you."

"Shall I pay now?"

"No, Jacob. On the house today. Let me treat the both of you."

"No way. I insist on paying."

"And I refuse your money. Go. Sit. I will be right over with your order."

"Ugh." Jacob sighed as we walked over to the table that Deanna picked out.

It did not take long for Stacy to make the ice creams. She brought both over and placed them on the table in front of Jacob and Deanna.

"Enjoy." Smiling, she walked away. She knew how much it drove Jacob crazy when someone treated him, but she knew he deserved it. Working hard, keeping an eye on his friend and her daughter, life was just a bit rough for him and a break was in order.

Jacob and Deanna sat in silence as they ate their ice cream. At one point Deanna had to stop due to a brain freeze. They both giggled at her expense. The last time Deanna was here, getting ice cream, was with her father.

*****

"Hey kid. Before we go get Mommy, let us get some ice cream. I could really use a cone."

"Okay, Dad. Let's go."

Eli drove the truck to the shop. Pulling up, he looked at his young daughter, popping her head back and forth to the song. How did he get so lucky?

"Hey, Dad."

"Yeah, kiddo."

"Why were you and Mommy yelling in the bedroom?"

"That's not for you to worry about."

"But that's all you do anymore. The yelling. You don't think I hear you, but I do, even with your door shut."

"Kiddo, Mommy and I, we are not agreeing on things right now. Don't you worry about it. We are trying to fix it. Let's get our cones."

"How can I not worry?" Deanna whispered. Eli pretended not to hear it. "Okay."

*****

"Dee. Dee. You okay?" Jacob noticed Deanna staring off into space.

"Oh, yeah."

"Want to talk about it?"

"Last time I was here was with my dad." Her eyes started to water. "Jacob, I asked my dad about the yelling. Was my mom and dad having troubles?"

56

"What do you mean, Dee?"

"Every night they would go into their room and shut the door. You can hear my mom yelling at my dad. She would be crying. My dad would be saying, 'I am sorry.' What were they fighting about?"

"Dee, this is something your mom needs to tell you."

"Do you know?"

"Yes, actually I do. I just never said anything. Your mom does not even remember I know. Your father confided in me."

"Please tell me. Mommy will not. I don't want to ask her."

"Deanna, you're just thirteen years old. This is not for you to worry about."

"You say I act older."

"You do, but I do not think it is my place to tell you."

"Please. Please, tell me."

"Your mom and dad were fighting. They were working on their marriage, but your mom could not trust your dad anymore. Trust is a big thing for her. Your father broke it. Just before the accident, they had started to fix it."

"How did he break her trust?"

"Dee."

"How?"

"I am not going into detail unless your mother wants me to."

"Please."

"No. It is not my place. You need to ask her."

It was not in his place to tell her that her father came to him, to ask him for forgiveness. He had a weak moment; he cheated on his wife, on Jacob's one true love. His secretary came into his office, and one thing led to another, and well, the door became locked and the desk became the spot.

*****

"Jacob, can you, um, meet me at the bench by the water fountain?"

"Yeah, Eli, everything okay?"

"Not really. I need to talk to you."

"Okay, I am on my way. I will see you in a second."

Jacob drove around the block to the park. Getting out, he saw Eli pacing back and forth.

"Yo, man, what's up?"

"I messed up big time, man! Big time! I need to ask you not to punch my face in first before I tell you."

"What did you do?"

"More like who did I do?"

"What! Don't tell me you fooled around?"

"With Tabby."

"ARE YOU KIDDING ME?"

"No, I wish I were. It just happened in my office."

"Just one time?"

"No, a few times. I just do not know what happened, what came over me."

"Dude, you have to come clean with Mary."

"I can't. It will kill her!"

"You have to, man, and you have to end it with Tabby!"

"I did. I told her I was married to an amazing woman, that I would transfer her over to another position."

"You have to tell Mary!"

"I can't. She will never forgive me. She will never trust me again."

"You tell her before I do! I am not kidding, Eli. You really messed up big time!"

"Why did I do it, man?"

"Eli, come clean with her. She will forgive you in time if she hears it from you and not me. Me, on the other hand, I am not happy with you. You promised me you would not hurt her, break her heart. This is going to shatter her!"

"I know, I know. I feel like an ass, Jacob. I really do. I am sorry."

"Well, you are one. Go. Go right now and tell her. I will pick Deanna up from school."

"You can't. You're on shift."

"I can and I will."

"Don't make her sit in the back of the squad car, dude."

"Ha! You don't want her to experience your mishaps."

"Not funny."

"No, I won't do that to her. She can sit in the front with me. Now GO. *Go break Mary's heart."*

*****

"Come on, Dee. Let's go see your mom." Jacob put his head down.

"Okay." Deanna dropped the subject. Getting up from the table, she followed Jacob out to the truck. "Thank you for taking me to get ice cream by the way."

"Dee, it was my pleasure." Jacob smiled.

He could not be the one to tell her that her father was unfaithful to her mother. Breaking news like that could destroy a child, let alone one that has already been through so much. He turned the radio on and drove off.

Deanna must have forgotten she was in Jacob's truck. As they listened to the radio, a Christian station, a beautiful rendition of "The Old Rugged Cross" came on. She had her eyes closed as she sang line for line, verse by verse.

"And I'll cherish the old rugged cross... Till my trophies at last I lay down. And I will cling to the old rugged cross...and exchanged it some day for a crown. I will cling to the old rugged cross... And exchange it some day for a crown."

"Wow, Dee. That was absolutely beautiful." Jacob, in astonishment, looked over at her.

"Oh, I... I am sorry. I forgot I was not alone."

"Don't be sorry. You have such a beautiful voice. Why don't I hear you sing with the church choir?"

"I just sing to myself usually."

"Well, you should sing so others can hear you. Does your mom know about your beautiful voice?"

"I don't think so."

"Well, since we are here, I think you should show her."

"No, thanks."

"Okay. You may not show her, but I am bragging about it." Jacob smirked as he got out of the truck.

"What, wait, no." Deanna swung the door open but not quick enough as Jacob was already at the doors to the salon.

"Okay, okay, I won't say anything here, but you know I will tell your mother just how amazing of a daughter she has."

"Ugh, whatever." Deanna walked past as he held the door open.

"Hey there, Deanna."

"Hey, Jenn."

"How are you?"

"Just fine. Have you seen my mom anywhere?"

"She is in the back but wants you and Jacob to wait up here for the big reveal."

"She really did it?" Jacob looked toward the back.

"Oh yeah. Her long brown hair is, well, wait till you see. She is just fixing her makeup."

Jacob and Deanna walked over the reception area. Deanna sat down, looking at a magazine, as Jacob walked around the room. Photos hung on the wall; one in particular was of a couple and young girl. Why haven't he notice that one before? Where has he seen it? The house. That is a photo just like on the mantel: her parents and her. He took a deep breath, trying to hold back the emotions that he felt when he was there until he saw her walking from the back. His heart fluttered. His eyes filled with joyful moisture that he pushed back. Her long legs were showing just a little, with her cute little butterfly-patterned dress. Her hair was no longer past her butt but shoulder-length. No longer a deep brown, but more of a chocolate color.

Mary's eyes locked onto Jacob's. The feeling she once had as a school girl, the fluttering, nervousness feeling took her breath away. Taking a deep breath, she walked up to Deanna and Jacob.

"Hello" was all that Jacob could get out.

CHAPTER 5

Mary Ann

"Jacob, are you sure?" Natalie started to cut away MaryAnn's hair.

"Yep, very sure." Mary took a deep breath. "What am I going to do?"

"Does he still feel the same way? I mean, that man has never gotten married and any relationship didn't work out. They would end it on a positive note but never move forward."

"I am certain I am the reason he never pushed forward."

"Well, one thing is certain: you cannot act on it, not just yet. You just lost your husband."

"My unfaithful husband."

"Be that it may, he was still your husband and Jacob's best friend. You two were working things out, weren't you?"

"We were trying to fix things. I love him. Do not get me wrong, but I could not trust him. He shattered me."

"Right now, you need a friend, not a romance. So just keep your friendship with Jacob. Let things play out. Let things move at its own pace. Pray over it."

"I knew you would say that. I asked him why they patrol the empty house."

"Your house. Girl, I know you from the homeschooling days. I know that is your house."

"My house of the past."

"That you still sit in front of often. Don't forget I live on that very street."

"I can never fool you."

"No, you cannot. So what did he say?"

"That captain has them maintaining the house. He did not go into too much detail; he does not know it is my house of the past. But the captain, he does. Mark was there, that day. He told me about my parents, and he stayed until my grandparents came for me. He was there when we laid my parents to rest. He has been there ever since. I am surprised he has not told Jacob. You know, he is Jacob's mentor."

"Maybe he feels it's your story to tell."

"Maybe."

"Just promise me, you will let it play out."

"I promise. Now, will you just dry my hair? I want to see it." Mary started to grow impatient. "They will be here soon. He is taking Dee out for ice cream."

"Aw, that is so sweet of him." Natalie turned the dryer on.

MaryAnn closed her eyes, getting lost in her thoughts. She knows Natalie is right. She needs to give herself some time. Time to heal. The death of Eli opened up the wound of losing her parents in the same tragic way. She needs to pull herself together. She knows, although he was unfaithful, they were trying to rebuild their relationship, if not for themselves, but for their daughter. Her daughter. How could she been so selfish? She needs to make sure her daughter is all right. She lost her father. Mary understood that feeling all too well. The tears started to fall. Natalie noticed the change in the air.

"Why the tears?"

"I am a selfish person."

"No, no you're not. MaryAnn, why would you say such a thing? You are not selfish. You are the most caring person I have ever known."

"I have been too depressed for myself, not even thinking about how Deanna lost a father."

"Look, I do not know one person who has gone through the hell you have gone through. Losing your parents so young, being uprooted, losing your grandparents, then getting married to a man who will later be unfaithful, then die the exact same way as your parents. I am surprised we have not committed you yet. So you may have been depressed, but your daughter, she understands more than you give her credit for. She lost her father, yes, but she is more worried to lose you now too. So stop. You are not selfish. You will be selfish if you do not take care of you and if you do not snap back, now knowing how your daughter feels."

"Committed?" MaryAnn started to chuckle. "You are the definition of a true friend."

"Out of all that, that's what you heard." Natalie shook her head as she applied the finishing touches.

"No, I heard it all, especially committed." Still chuckling, MaryAnn wiped her eyes.

"I can't with you." Shaking her head, Natalie turned the chair around. "What do you think of my masterpiece?"

"Oh, my goodness, I look like a whole new me."

"With runny mascara." Natalie pointed out, walking away. "Here, fix your face. They are here."

"Really?"

"Yep."

"Excuse me, MaryAnn, Jacob and Deanna are here and just wow. I love it!"

"Shh, Jenn. Thanks. Do not tell anyone. I want to reveal it to Deanna. Let me just fix my makeup."

"Okay, I will tell them to stay out there."

"Thanks." MaryAnn grabbed the makeup and started to apply a fresh coat. "The highlights and low lights, the caramel with the chocolate. You outdid yourself! Make sure to take a photo of the color. We can definitely advertise this."

"Always in the business mind frame. Just enjoy it. Enjoy your evening."

"I am planning to take Deanna out for dinner."

"Just Deanna?"

"Jacob and I, we are going out tomorrow night. We need to fix our friendship. Things got weird after he confessed to me about who he truly was."

"Why wait till tomorrow?"

"Why do it in front of Deanna?"

"No, no. Why wait till tomorrow for dinner? Why discuss it? Why not let things just flow into place? Like it never happened."

"But it did."

"It did, indeed, but why act on it, is all I am saying. God will guide you two together if that is his plans."

"And if it is not?"

"Then you two will have the most magical friendship we could all hope for. Now go, strut your stuff in that cute butterfly dress."

"I can't believe you convinced me to put this on by the way."

"It looks good on you. Now your hair is done, your makeup is fixed. Get out of here."

MaryAnn shot a look at Natalie, only to give her a deep hug.

"Thank you, thank you for everything."

"Anytime, girl, anytime. Now go!"

MaryAnn walked from around the back of the salon. Everyone stopped what they were doing and just looked. The transformation had everyone in awe. She paid no mind to the ladies in the room. Her eyes locked on to Jacob's. He stood there, not breathing, mouth slightly open, and his eyes glistened. Taking a deep breath, she took one step at a time until she was in front of him.

"Hello."

"Hey, Jacob." Finally, words exited out of her mouth after a few seconds' delay.

"You look amazing."

"Thanks." Her cheeks blushed.

"Mommy...is that you?" Deanna broke through their thoughts.

"What do you think, Dee?"

"Wow, Mommy, you look very beautiful." Deanna walked up and hugged her mother. "I really like it."

"Me too, baby girl, me too." Hugging her daughter back, Mary looked back over at Jacob.

"I will go and let you two have your night."

"Hey, Jacob. I would like, I mean, if you have nothing going on tonight, to join us. Come have dinner with us."

"I don't want to intrude on your mother-and-daughter night."

"No, Jacob, join us," Deanna perked up. "It will be fun."

"Are you sure?"

"Yes. Come with us." Mary reached for Jacob's arm. "We would love to have you there."

"Okay, since you insist, I would love to join you two."

"Then it's settled. Where are we going?"

"Can we go to the pizza place?" Deanna spoke up.

"Sure. How's that sound, Jacob?"

"Sounds perfect. How about I drive us?"

"Great." MaryAnn pushed her hair behind her ear. "Nat, thanks for everything," she shouted as they headed for the door.

Pushing the door open, Jacob held it as the girls walked out. Taking a deep breath, he grabbed the passenger side door, opening it for Mary to get in, following the back door for Deanna to climb in.

The pizza place was not that far away, a quick ten-minute drive, yet the conversation that took place made it feel more like an hour.

"Mom, can I ask you something without you getting mad?"

"Why would I get mad?"

"Mom."

"Okay. Go ahead and ask."

"Last time Daddy took me to get ice cream, I asked him a question and he would not answer it."

"What did you ask him?"

"Why you two were always yelling. What happened between you and Daddy?"

"Deanna, I really do not want to answer that."

"Please, Mom. Jacob told me, it had to come from you. So I know it's bad."

"Jacob?" Mary looked over at him. "You know?" Forgetting that very night, that Jacob went to look for her. The night Eli came clean.

"Eli confided in me. It was not my place to tell you, but had he not, I was going to. I gave him no choice."

"What?" MaryAnn's mind was racing. "I thought you were—"

"Like I said, Mary. I told him, the moment he told me, if he did not come clean with you that day, if he did not stop this fool-

65

ishness, I was coming over to tell you. It is not like I was not going to tell you. It was not in my place, just as it is not in my place to answer Deanna's question. She heard you two fighting every night." Speaking up before she even finished her sentence, Jacob looked over into her eyes. "I think she has the right to know."

"Deanna, if I tell you what was going on, promise me, it won't change what you thought of your father. He was your hero and I do not want to change it."

"Mom, what did he do? Did he steal? Did he commit a crime?"

"In God's eyes he did." MaryAnn took a deep breath. "Dee, Daddy had an affair with his assistant for almost a year. Jacob, I totally forgot that night you found me, telling me you knew."

*****

"Mary, we need to talk." Eli walked in the door.

"Okay, well, do you want to help me finish dinner up first?" MaryAnn grabbed the chicken from the oven.

"Mary, we need to talk." Eli looked down at the floor.

"I know, you said that already." Wearing the oven mitts, she moved the chicken to the table. "What is going on, Eli? Did something happen to Deanna? Did something happen to Jacob?"

"No, they are okay. Deanna is outside, where I told her to stay, until we were done talking."

"Oh. Okay." MaryAnn's eyes grew wide. Something terrible was bothering her husband. "Let's sit down."

Eli followed MaryAnn to the living room, where she sat on one couch and he chose to sit on the other.

"Mary, you know I love you so very much. You changed me, made me better. You're an amazing wife, mother, and business owner."

"Eli, you're starting to scare me."

"Please, let me finish. This is hard to get out." He finally looked up at her. "Mary, for almost eight months or so, I have been having an affair with my assistant."

"What?" MaryAnn could not believe the words she was hearing. Her eyes filled with moisture.

"*I am so, so sorry, Mary.*"

"*I just don't understand, Eli. Why, just why would you do this?*"

"*I don't know, Mary.*"

Mary put her face into her hands. Tears overflowing. Eli went to sit next to her, to wrap his arms around her.

"*No! No! YOU DO NOT GET TO COME NEAR ME!*" *Anger filled her lungs as she stood up.*

"*Mary, I want to fix this. I don't want to lose you.*"

"*No, too late for that! There is no coming back from what you did. I can forgive, that is what the Lord teaches us, but you, I cannot forget what you did. DO NOT touch me. I can't even look at you right now.*"

"*Mary.*"

"*No! Eli, NO!*" *Wiping her eyes, MaryAnn took a deep breath.* "*You broke our vow! If you wanted to fix it, fix us, you would have not done this. What about our daughter, Eli? What about Deanna? What is this going to do to her? ELI, you are her hero!*"

"*What do you want me to do, Mary? I said I was sorry. I said I regret it. I said I want to fix this. What do you want me to do?*"

"*You did enough, Eli. You did enough. I need to go for a walk. I need to clear my head.*" *Mary grabbed her phone, headed for the door.*

"*Are you coming back?*"

"*OF course, I am.*" *She shot him a glare.* "*Unlike you, I do not abandon my family.*"

Stepping outside, she found Deanna sitting on the porch.

"*Are you guys okay?*"

"*Yes. I am going for a walk. I need to think some things through. I want you to go inside, get ready for dinner and bed. I will be back. You can start dinner without me. It is ready and on the table. You just have to get the carrots from the stove.*"

"*Mom, where are you going? It is getting dark.*"

"*For a walk, Dee, for a walk.*"

Deanna watched her mother walk away. Heading inside, she found her father, watching out the window.

"*Dad, why is Mom upset? Why is she taking a walk"?*

"*We had a disagreement. Just go wash your hands and get ready for dinner.*"

"She said to go ahead and start to eat without her."

"What?"

"Mom said to go ahead and start eating."

"Go ahead in the kitchen. I will be there in a moment." Eli watched Deanna head to the kitchen as he grabbed his phone.

"Jacob here."

"Jake, I told her. She walked out, went for a walk."

"I don't blame her. You shattered her. You broke her heart."

"I told her I was sorry. I told her I regretted it. What more can I do? And do not say you could have never done it. It is done. I can't go back in time and change what I did."

"What do you want me to do? She needs to go for a walk and clear her head."

"Go be her friend that she needs. Please just patrol the neighborhood, make sure she is okay. It is getting dark out. She told Deanna to come in for dinner and go ahead and eat without her. That is not Mary. She always is there. She says grace."

"Well, you just flipped her world as she knows it, man. Knowing her tragic past and you still flipped her world."

"Please, just patrol the neighborhood."

"Fine. I am not bringing her home unless she asks me to." Jacob hung up the phone and turned the cruiser around. Driving slowly, he turned down one road after another, looking for Mary. Ten minutes passed; Jacob started to grow a little worried. Just as he reached for his phone to call her, he spotted a figure in the dark shadow, slowly walking. Slowing down, he rolled his window down.

"Hey, pretty lady."

Looking up, she wiped her eyes. Jacob saw that she had been crying. Putting the cruiser in park, he got out. Walking over, not saying a word, he just wrapped his arms around her, holding her.

"I am sorry, I am sorry he did this to you."

"You know?"

"He confided in me today. I told him, he had to come clean with you or I was, and it would be more respectful if you heard it from him."

"Jacob, what is wrong with me?"

"Nothing, Mary, nothing at all. Why would you ask that?"

"Why else would he cheat? Something has to be wrong with me. Am I no longer attractive? Am I no longer entertaining?"

He pulled her away from his chest, taking his hand and tilting her head up so their eyes would meet.

"Mary, you are the most beautiful woman I have ever seen, from the inside out. Do not let him change you, take that from you. He is the one that has the issues. He is the one with the problems."

"He said he wanted to fix this, but I don't think I can. I can't let him touch me with those hands, the hands and mouth that was all over her."

"You are going to pray. That is what we do. Cast all your cares upon Him. First Peter 5:7 states, 'Casting all your care upon him; for he careth for you.' The Lord will hold you up."

"Jacob, I don't know if I can."

"You can, you will try. I know this."

"How?"

"Because I know you are a woman of faith. You will try to mend a broken wheel even if there is no way to mend it. You will push for your family because you love your family. Even though you are hurt, you love your family. That is just the person you are. You are beautiful, strong, amazing—the complete package. Eli will, I pray that he does anyway, fight for you because you are worth fighting for even when mistakes have been made."

MaryAnn broke down, tears falling as she began to fall to her knees, only to be caught in Jacob's arms.

"Why can't he be more like you? Why can't he see me the way you do?" Sobbing, she grabbed on to his shoulders.

"I don't know, Mary. The only thing I do know is that deep down inside he does love you. So hang on to that, okay?"

"Okay."

"Do you want me to take you home?"

MaryAnn looked around, looking for a street sign.

"I walked ten blocks?" Confused, she looked back at Jacob. "I don't even know how I did that. I just left and started to walk."

"That happens. Let me take you home. Deanna is very worried about you, and believe it or not so is Eli."

"I just can't believe... I thought I just walked around the block."

"Let me take you home, Mary."

"Okay, Jacob."

Without warning, Jacob shifted Mary off her feet and into his arms, carrying her to the front seat of his police cruiser. Sitting her down, he then radioed in, letting dispatch know he is out of commission until further notice. Sliding into the driver's seat, he took Mary's hand.

"Mary, you will be okay. I am here for you. You're not alone."

"Thank you, Jacob. That means the world to me."

*****

Taking a deep breath, MaryAnn turned around in her seat, looked at Deanna. Taking her hand, she looked into her teary blue eyes.

"Your father loved you very much."

"He loved your mother too," Jacob spoke up.

"Not as much as other's though," MaryAnn whispered as she looked over at Jacob. "He just had a time of weakness."

"Why would he do that??" Deanna wiped her eyes.

"Deanna, I have known your father since we were babies. He was always the crazy, wild child who had his own set ways. The day your mother came into his life was the day his life was changed for the better. Your mom got him to go to church, something I tried so hard to get him to do. She got him to settle down. Sometimes, when the devil knows your weakness, he will prey on it and send in someone else to do his job, such as flirt, make passes, pull at an old habit."

"Why couldn't he just say, 'No, I am happily married, with a family'? I just do not understand."

"We don't either, Dee." MaryAnn shook head.

"Mom, what did you mean when you whispered, 'Not as much as others'?"

"I just meant he didn't love me enough not to cheat. He loved me, just not enough." Looking up at Jacob, Mary quickly looked back down.

He knows she was referring the love he has for her and always had. Taking a deep breath, things are surely different now she knows who he truly is. Yet he still cannot and will not act on it. She is the widow of his best friend, his very stupid best friend.

"If you guys were trying to fix it, why did you fight so much every single night?"

"I was hurt. No matter how hard I prayed, it was extremely hard to forgive him. He made me feel worthless, he made me feel ugly." She was trying to keep it so that her daughter would understand just a little bit. "So when he tried to kiss me, touch me, I couldn't remove her face from my memory. So I would push him away, which would anger him, then in return would anger me, for he was the reason for the fall."

"How am I supposed to not be angry with him right now?"

"You can be angry with your father, Dee. Just don't stay angry with him for long. Anger will tear you down, like it tore our marriage further apart." Taking a deep breath, she continued, "I should have learned to tame my anger sooner. By the time I started to let it go, move on, he died."

Deanna reached over the truck seat and hugged her mother. They sat there for some time in silence. Then both of them were in tears. Jacob sat back and gave them their space.

"I am going to give you two some space and step out of the truck," Jacob spoke in a low whispered tone as he stepped out of the truck.

Hearing the door shut, they both looked up.

"I guess, now the cat is out of the bag, we can go eat. I am starving," MaryAnn softly spoke. "I didn't want to tell you about it, but you deserve to know. I didn't want to be the cause of your feelings against your father."

"Mom, somehow, some way it would have gotten back to me, eventually."

"I know. I know."

"Mom, can I ask you something else?"

"I don't know, Dee. The last question was deep."

"Can we eat? I am starving, and Jacob is waiting for us."

"Silly girl, yes, let's go out. Poor guy is leaning against his own truck."

Jacob looked back, seeing the passenger's door opening; he quickly walked over to open it all the way.

"Thank you, Jacob, for giving us space."

"You are welcome." He smiled as he reached his hand out. MaryAnn placed her hand into his as she slid out of the truck, only to let go once she was out and standing up.

"So, ladies, what are we going to eat?" Jacob opened the door into the pizza parlor.

"Pizza of course," Deanna spoke up.

"Hi. Welcome. How are we today?" The hostess, with long beautiful brown hair, batted her brown eyes toward Jacob.

"Hi, we are fine and in need of a seat for three please." MaryAnn saw the flirtatious movement; her hair on the back of her neck stood, giving the hostess a glare, making her turn her face.

"Three. Booth or table?"

"Booth in the corner would be best." Not letting up, MaryAnn spoke up.

"Booth in the corner it is." She grabbed three menus and led the way.

Jacob slid in the booth as Mary slid in next to him, allowing Deanna to sit across from them both. The hostess dropped the menus off without looking at Jacob anymore and walked away.

"Um, what just happened there?" Jacob whispered into Mary's ear.

"Mom, I am going to go to the bathroom. Can we get sausage on our pizza?"

"Sure thing, kiddo." Mary watched Deanna get up and walk to the bathroom before responding to Jacob. "The hostess just rubbed me the wrong way. How does she know if we are together or not and had the nerve to flirt and bat her eyes?"

"Well, you know how I feel, and although our paths have not crossed in that way, you have nothing to worry about."

"That's not fair to you though. Maybe one day, our paths will cross that way, but it is still not fair for you."

"Maybe, but I find it cute the way you reacted." Jacob placed his hand onto hers and kissed it so slightly. "You don't have to worry about me."

"Hey there, Jacob."

"Hey, Joel."

"Good evening there, MaryAnn. Is Deanna with us too?"

"She sure is. Do we have the pleasure of the owner waiting on us tonight?"

"Well, you scared off my waitress, so yep." Joel looked at MaryAnn with a chuckle.

"Oh. I am sorry, Joel. She—"

"Flirts way too much, something I already had a talk with her about. No worries. I saw you two when I came up to the front. I rather wait on my friends."

"Hi, Joel." Deanna walked up behind him.

"Hey there, Dee. Are we getting our normal sausage pizza with extra cheese?"

"Mom?"

"Yes, Joel, that would be perfect."

"What to drink?"

"Water for Deanna and me please," MaryAnn spoke up with her pink rosy cheeks.

"I will take a water as well please." Jacob smiled.

"Water all around with a large extra cheese and sausage pie. Your drinks will be out momentarily."

"Thanks, Joel."

"You are welcome." Joel walked away.

"So how was school today, Dee?"

"It was good. I passed my test. I was thinking of joining the Bible club. They start up in January."

"Oh, that sounds awesome. Is it something new?"

"Yes."

MaryAnn could not help but to smile. It has been a very long time since she has seen Deanna bright and cheerful, let alone for herself to be out of the house. She watched Deanna and Jacob, in a deep conversation about what clubs are offered now and what clubs were offered when he was in school. They paused as the waitress brought the waters.

"Three waters." She handed MaryAnn one, sat the second one in front of MaryAnn, and handed Deanna hers. "The pie will be out shortly."

"Thank you." MaryAnn looked at her.

"You're welcome." She quickly turned and walked away.

"Well, I guess this water is yours." MaryAnn chuckled as she handed Jacob the water.

"Well, I know if I come in here on my own, I will have to fend for myself." He shook his head as he returned the laughter. Deanna just sat there, looking confused.

"Scoot over, Dee." Joel came over to the table with the pie. "I figure I would join you today. This pie is on the house tonight."

"No, no. Joel, we can pay for it."

"Nonsense, Jacob. The owner says it's on the house." Joel was happy to see both MaryAnn and Deanna smiling, something the whole town has not seen for some time now.

"So, MaryAnn, new hair to go with that brand-new smile? Nat gave me a call, told me she was so happy you came into the salon today and got a total makeover."

"So she is bragging."

"Well, of course, she is. We all have been so worried about you and Deanna."

"Well, for the first time in a long time, I feel good, alive. When you have friends who do not let up, when you have a daughter who says the right words, and when you pray, things start to make a better turn. We are going to start going through Eli's things, his clothes, and donate them, maybe even paint the house, change it up. Make it refreshed. We are not going to forget him, but he would want us to live our life. Right, Dee?"

"Yep." She just shoved a piece of pizza into her mouth.

"Well, that is what we like to hear. You do have a really good friend by your side, Jacob."

"I know. He is truly the best." MaryAnn looked up into Jacob's eyes, sparks flying, taking her breath away. Still she was not too sure on acting on them. Eli just passed away, and they were best of friends. Jacob made it clear that he was Eli's best friend, first and foremost. She quickly turned her face from his.

"Mom, why is your face so red?" Deanna spoke up in innocence.

"It's warm in here." Coming up with a quick excuse, MaryAnn's face grew even more of a red. "Excuse me while I use the ladies' room." Quickly she got up and went to put some nice cool water onto her face.

"Deanna, why don't you go check on your mom? I want to chat with Jacob."

"Okay, Joel."

Deanna moved out from the booth and headed to the bathroom.

"What are you doing?"

"What do you mean, Joel?"

"I see the way you two look at each other."

"We are friends. I was her husband's best friend. That is it. We are not involved or any of those sorts."

"Answer me this, honestly. Nat always spoke how you could not make things work with the other girls because some girl from your senior year stole your heart. Is that girl Mary?"

"How do you know? Did Cap say something?"

"It is obvious. You always went about and beyond for her, even when Eli was alive. Now even more. I know it is what friends do. It is the godly thing to do. But nobody, no friend, looks at her the way you do, and let me tell you no friend looks at you the way she does."

"Nothing could ever come out of it, Joel. She is the widow of my best friend. There is a code."

"A code that he broke when he had an affair. The whole town knew about it. Nobody said anything for Deanna's sake. Look, do not say nothing could ever come out of it. I think in time, when it's right, you two should venture down that path. I think it would be the best thing for the both of you. A happy ending to one messed up book. You both deserve it. Boy, you're like a son to me, so trust me."

"Well, this is some serious conversation we are walking up on," MaryAnn chimed in.

"More like a father talking to a young lad I helped raise in some way or form."

"Well, if you're going to put him over your knee for a good whooping, let me get my phone so I can record it." MaryAnn laughed along with Deanna.

"Not right." Jacob snickered.

"What?" Throwing her hands up in a joking manner, MaryAnn slid in next to Jacob.

The rest of the night was filled with laughter, jokes, stories of the past. Before they knew it, it was time to leave. Jacob, a gentleman as always, held the doors open for Deanna and Mary as well as opened the passenger's side door for them both. Reaching the salon, he made sure to park right next to MaryAnn's car.

"Let me get your door." He put his truck into park, turning off the engine.

"You do not have to get out. We can open the door, Jacob."

"I know you can, but it would not be right of me to allow you to do that." Jacob quickly got out of the truck and walked to her door, just as MaryAnn opened it. "It is the right thing to do. A gentleman should always open the door, no matter what door it is, for a lady. That goes for you too, Deanna. When you start dating, keep one thing in mind. See how he treats his mother, sisters, grandmothers, aunts, and so on. If he treats them with respect, dignity, then he was raised right and, in the long run, will treat you good."

"Jacob is right, Dee. My mother once told me that the summer before I started high school. I totally forgot about it until now."

"You don't talk about your parents much, Mom."

"I know. I am sorry. One day, we will sit, and I will tell you all that I can remember."

MaryAnn got out, stepping aside to allow Jacob to open Deanna's door.

"Jacob, thank you for picking me up and coming to dinner with Mommy and I. Thank you for being there as I asked Mommy about Daddy."

"Dee, you don't fool me. That's why you asked me to stay, for dinner, to be a buffer." Jacob smiled as he gave her a hug. "You're welcome. Just as I am here for your mom, I am here for you as well."

Deanna returned the hug and walked over to her mother's car. MaryAnn hit the unlock button, allowing Deanna to get in out of the darkness.

"Jacob, you are truly an amazing person and my best friend. Thank you for telling me the truth, about everything. Thank you for stepping aside to let Eli know what love is. Thank you for always being there then and now. I just do not know what I would do without you." She wrapped her arms around his waist and pulled him in for a tight hug.

In return, he wrapped his arms around her, holding her tightly.

"There is no need to thank me, Mary. I will forever be here for you, no matter what. If something changes for us or not, I will always be here for you and Deanna. No matter what."

CHAPTER 6

New Beginnings

The morning sun peeked through the curtains. No need to rush to get out of bed. Saturday mornings, no school, no rush to get up. Today is the day, MaryAnn decided, to clean out Eli's clothing. You cannot move on from the past if you are still holding on to it. Having his clothes in their bedroom is a daily reminder that he is not coming home although it has not been a home for a long time.

"Mom, are you awake?" Deanna knocked on the door.

"I am. You can come in."

"I just want to know if you would like some cereal. Or waffles."

"What are you having?"

"Not too sure."

"Well, why don't I get out of bed, make us some eggs?"

"That sounds good."

"Hey, Dee. Can you help me bag up Daddy's things?"

"Sure."

"I would like to start redoing the house." MaryAnn sat up as she kicked her legs over the edge of the bed. "What colors should we paint?"

"Can we do two colors in my room? Like teal and gray?"

"That would be a pretty combo. What about my room? Pale pink and gray?"

"Oh, I like that, Mom. What about earth tones for the living room?"

"Like the hall a light tan, sandy?"

"Yeah. And a sea green for the living room, or maybe the tan for the living room and the sea green for the hallway."

"Dee, I like that idea. What would you think about just taking this wall down and making the living room more open, flowing into the kitchen and dining room?"

"Think Jacob would know how to do that?"

"I don't know. We can always call and ask him."

"Already on it, Mom." Dee took out her cellphone. Clicking on his contact, she hit the call button.

"Dee, its early. He might be working or sleeping."

"Jacob."

"Dee, what's wrong? Everything okay? Your mom okay?"

"We are fine. I am sorry. I didn't mean to worry you."

"It's okay. You never call. What's up? Why are you up so early?"

"Mom and I, we are getting ready to have some breakfast, and we were talking about the house. Can you knock a wall down?"

"Dee, you should ask if you are bothering him first," MaryAnn spoke from the kitchen.

"Tell your mom you're not bothering me. I was just watching the news and having coffee, and no, I am not at work, before she asks that."

"Nope, Mom, he is good."

"So to answer your question, yes, I can knock down the wall, depending if it's low bearing or not."

"What is that?"

"Why don't I just come over?"

"Good idea. Want eggs? Mom is cooking."

"I would love some eggs. Just warn your mom that I am on the way so she can get dressed. I know she doesn't like to be seen in her pajamas."

"Okay. See you soon." Deanna hung the phone up. "Mom, Jacob is on the way. He said to tell you so you can get dressed. He is off today and wants to look at the wall you want down to make sure it is not bearing, high...no, low... I do not remember. He said he would love some eggs."

MaryAnn just looked at Deanna, eyes wide.

"Okay, let me get dressed." MaryAnn headed toward her room. "You know you could have waited to call him."

"I know." Deanna headed to her room to get out of her pajamas as well. "But why wait?"

"I do not know what I am going to do with you." MaryAnn went into her room, searching for the right pair of leggings and shirt. She grabbed the black leggings and her stripped gray shirt. Just as she pulled it over her head, she heard the doorbell ring.

"Hey, Jacob." Deanna answered the door. "Mom is still getting dressed."

"No, I am here. Dee, how many eggs do you want?"

"Two please."

"Jacob?"

"Two please and let me help you with the bacon."

"Bacon? We only have eggs."

"Nope, I brought bacon." He held up a pack of bacon. "You cook the eggs and I will cook the bacon."

"Sounds like a plan."

"As we cook, tell me your plans for the house?"

MaryAnn grabbed the deep-frying pan, handing it to Jacob. She grabbed her smaller one and stood right next to him to start the eggs.

"I brought bread too. Deanna, why don't you start toasting some bread?" Jacob pointed to the loaf of bread on the table.

"Okay." Deanna grabbed the loaf. "Two for each?"

"Yes, so that would be two times three."

"Six. That was so easy, Jacob."

"Well then." He laughed as he started to put the bacon in the hot pan. "So what wall are we knocking down?"

"Well, I was thinking that one. That separates the living room from the kitchen and dining room."

"That might be a low bearing. We just might have to reenforce it."

"I don't think it is. When Eli and I bought the house, he had the wall put up to separate the room. I liked it open."

"That is right. I was away on training that weekend when he asked me for help. So then it is already reenforced. So yeah, let's knock it down. We can start today. I have the whole weekend off."

"Wait, are you sure? I don't want to waste your weekend, Jacob."

"Yeah, I am sure. Let's knock this puppy down. What else are we doing?"

"Packing Eli's clothes up to donate, painting rooms, rearranging, and eventually I want to buy new furniture. Really, redo this house. Freshen it up."

"Goodness, by time you're done with all of this, your house will look brand-new, unrecognizable."

"That's the idea." MaryAnn knew he was pointing at the simple fact: redoing this house is taking Eli out of it. Maybe it's the wrong thing to do, but for her it's the right thing to do.

"Then let's do it." He placed the bacon on a big plate as MaryAnn began to place eggs, two by two, on separate plates. Jacob grabbed one plate at a time and placed them on the table.

"This is nice," Deanna spoke softly.

"What's that?" MaryAnn looked at her as she took her seat.

"This. Breakfast. Working together to cook. To sit. This is nice."

"Yes, it is, baby girl. Something I have missed, something you should have had. I am sorry you didn't." Eli never helped make any meal; he just came in, sat down, ate in silence, no talking. He did not like to talk at the table. Jacob looked at them as he took his seat.

"Let us bow. I will say grace." MaryAnn folded her hands and bowed her head. "Heavenly Father, thank you for this chance to start fresh. To push forward. Lord, we thank you for friendship, for family. I ask that you bless this amazing smelling breakfast and the rest of the day as it begins to unfold. May you continue to look after us as we take each day the way you want us to do. In Jesus Christ's name, we pray, Amen."

"Amen," Deanna and Jacob said together.

"Thank you for the bacon and bread."

"It is my pleasure, Mary. Thank you for the eggs. It is much nicer to eat in company instead of alone, that is for sure."

"I can see that."

"So, Dee. After breakfast, we can start the demo. Do you want to help your mom with bagging the clothes? Or do you want to take the photos and things off the wall and clear the chairs from the wall, and I will help your mom? If we tackle two things at a time, we can maybe paint by tomorrow."

"You can help Mommy."

"Wow, Jacob. I think you are more determined than I am at this point." MaryAnn smiled at him.

"I like doing makeovers." Jacob shrugged his shoulders. "So how many bags should I grab?"

"The whole box." MaryAnn was serious. She wanted to donate it all. Nothing left behind.

"Okay." Jacob grabbed his last bacon.

Breakfast soon came to an end. Jacob got up and started to clear the table.

"You know, we can do that. Why don't you relax? You are the guest."

"Yep, I am. I'll take your plate, thanks." He was smiling at her as he took her plate and placed it in the sink. "I will help you clean this up later. Deanna, why don't you start to clear the wall? Everything off and away from it. Mary, are you ready?"

Reaching out his hand, with the box of trash bags in his other hand, she placed her hand into his, helping her up. They walked hand in hand down the hall, not aware of Deanna watching their moves.

"I do not want to keep a thing. Just take and empty his drawers into the bags and his side of the closet too."

"Are you sure, Mary?"

"Frankly, I was only trying to fix the marriage because of Deanna. I love Eli, do not get me wrong. I forgave Eli, but I could not forget. Lord forgive me, but I just could not forget. I loved him, but I was not in love with him. Does that make any sense?"

"Yes, it makes total sense." He opened a bag and did just as she asked. One drawer at a time, one bag at a time. Mary worked on the closet. Every once in a while, Jacob would hear her sniffle. He knew she was still very much hurting not just from his death but also from the pain, knowing he had an affair numerous time.

"You know, Mary, the only time I have ever seen you lose your cool was at his funeral."

"I just could not believe she would even think to come to his funeral, show her face."

"Yeah, well the whole town knew who she was and what she did after that."

*****

"What are you doing here?" MaryAnn, eyes red and swollen from crying, firmly spoke to a long blonde-hair woman. "Again, what gives you any right to be here?"

"Cap, take Deanna out of here." Jacob sensed something was not right.

"Okay, Deanna, let's head to the limo. We are going to ride in that to the graveyard."

"Why can't I stay with my mom?"

"Go!" MaryAnn did not want her daughter here, around her. She pointed her finger to the door. Watching Captain Mark Shell escort her daughter out the door, she again looked into the woman's eyes. "YOU are NOT welcome here!"

"I just wanted to pay my respect to Eli."

"To the man you screwed on his desk, more than once, KNOWING HE HAS A FAMILY! You opened your legs to a married man. You do not get to pay respects to my husband! YOU NEED TO LEAVE!"

"I am so, so sorry."

"No, TABBY, YOU'RE NOT! YOU ARE SORRY YOU GOT CAUGHT!" MaryAnn started to yell. Everyone in the church turned to see the commotion. "YOU ARE SORRY HE TOLD YOU IT WAS OVER! GO FIND ANOTHER MARRIAGE TO BREAK UP, HOME-WRECKER!"

"Tabby, it is best that you leave. You should have never come!" Jacob placed his hand under MaryAnn's elbow. "Come on, Mary, let's follow Eli out."

"*Do not go to his grave, not now, not never!*" *MaryAnn continued on.*

"*If you kept your husband satisfied, he would not have wanted to have fun with me!*" *Tabby said in a snarky tone once she realized everyone was watching.*

Before Jacob could even grab MaryAnn, she raised her hand and slapped it right across Tabby's face, leaving a bright-red handprint. Jacob quickly pulled MaryAnn back.

"*How DARE YOU!*"

Natalie saw the commotion and ran up to Jacob and MaryAnn.

"*What is going on?*"

"*This is the home-wrecker that had an affair with Eli!*"

"*Come on, Mary.*" *Jacob started to pull her into him in order to guide her out of the church. "Get her out of here, Nat."*

"*Let's go, Tabby. You have done enough. Now the whole town knows what kind of person you are. Had you stayed away they would have never known it was you.*"

"*Natalie, I loved him.*"

"*Thank goodness Jacob has MaryAnn out of hearing. You would have had another handprint. Look, what you did is wrong, so very wrong. I suggest you just stay away, from her, from us all, from the grave site. I have never seen MaryAnn like that before, and I am afraid to see what else she will do to you. You fell in love with a married man. How horrible does that sound and for the simple fact you felt the need to make a scene at his funeral, in front of his family, everyone? Best that you leave.*" *Natalie escorted Tabby out the side door, away from MaryAnn and everyone else. The pastor followed as well.*

"*Tabby, I will pray for your lost soul,*" *the pastor spoke as she walked away. "Thank you, Natalie, for helping with that tough situation."*

"*No worries.*" *She turned and walked toward her car.*

*****

"I thought for sure you were going to knock her right out of her shoes. I think she is still feeling that sting."

"I should have hit her other side when she said she loved him. Nat thinks I didn't hear her, but I did, and you wouldn't loosen up."

"Imagine that I did. You would have knocked her into next month."

"Honestly, I do not know where that came from. I have never ever hit anyone, let alone yell at them."

"You needed that, Mary. You needed to say something that you were holding on to for far too long." Jacob tied up the last bag. "Four bags of clothes."

Mary grabbed the last shirt of his from the closet. Taking it, she remembered that was the shirt he was wearing when she met him, the shirt that he wore when he asked her to marry him. Anger built up in her. Her eyes filled with tears. Ripping the shirt off the hanger, she looked over at Jacob.

"How dare he? How dare he break us."

Jacob quickly dropped the bag on the floor and swiftly walked over to MaryAnn, wrapping her into his arms. She fell apart in them.

"Why did he do it? Why did he break us, break me?"

"I have you," Jacob whispered as she sobbed.

"Why couldn't I find you first?"

"We can't live with the whys or what ifs. We have to live for today and for tomorrow, not yesterday. Our paths are chosen for different reasons."

Deanna walked down the hall, wanting to tell Jacob that the wall was ready to come down—only to walk into the room, seeing him holding her mother as she cried in his arms. Jacob noticed Deanna staring at them. He mouthed, "It will be okay." She shook her head and stepped out of the room.

"Mary, look at me." Jacob tipped her chin up so he can look into her eyes. "You are not broke. You are wounded, yes, but not broke. You are beautiful, amazing, and the most wonderful mother. He was a complete fool. Let the past rest. Let's move forward. I never want to hear you say he broke you again because you are not broken. You are strong."

Looking up into his eyes, MaryAnn listened to his words, each of them. She could feel his chest rise with each breath, his heartbeat.

Not moving out of his hands, she continued to look into his eyes. He slowly wiped her tears off her cheeks. Unable to find her breath, she moved her chin up a little more, reaching her lips to his. Very softly, slowly, her lips parted, parting his. He returned the kiss. Her heart raced. Oh, how this truly felt right. Jacob slowed the kiss, retracting back, putting his forehead against hers.

"Oh, how I longed so long for that kiss," he said, whispering. "Mary, let's just take each day as they come. I pray that God brings us together when the time is right."

"Me too," she whispered. "Me too." She wrapped her arms tightly around him. Was it wrong of her to want more so soon?

"Well, how many bags did you get?"

"Three."

"So seven bags so far."

"I still have the hall closet. Then we can drop it off to the church on our way to the hardware store for the paint."

"That sounds like a great plan, Mary."

"And you're okay, wasting your day away with us?"

"I'm not wasting the day when I am with you, Mary. I enjoy being with you and Dee."

"Good because I enjoy having you here. Let's go see what Dee has completed." MaryAnn smiled. Everything felt right. Things were finally moving in the right direction.

"Dee, how are you doing?" Jacob came out.

"All the photos are off the wall. All the furniture is moved away from the wall, and I even started to pull the trim off."

"Well, good girl. Can you come help your mom and I load the truck up with the bags? We have one more closet to get, then we are heading to the store to pick paint, get supplies and heavy-duty containers for the wall debris."

"How many bags so far?"

"Seven, might end up being ten. So we can start to take them out while your mom finishes."

"I am glad you're here." Deanna surprised Jacob with a hug. MaryAnn just watched in awe.

"You're welcome, Dee, you are so welcome." He returned the hug. "Okay, kid, let's get moving. I want to make it back before the storms approach. My goal today is getting the wall down and floor and holes sealed up. Once that is done, we can prep to paint, then tomorrow we paint and paint and paint."

Deanna quickly grabbed a bag and headed out to the truck. Jacob followed in her footsteps, grabbing two bags. By the time they came back in from taking the last bags out, MaryAnn had another bag ready.

"I think we will surpass ten bags. He had so much crap." MaryAnn looked up with apology in her eyes.

"Well, someone will greatly benefit from it." Jacob grabbed the bag and handed it to Deanna.

"Mom, this makes eleven bags."

"I have one more. I am just about done." She grabbed a handful of clothes, taking them off the hangers and shoving them in the bags. "Moving forward with life may be difficult but it is healthy."

"I know, Mom. We will remember him in our hearts."

"Yes, baby girl. In our hearts."

"Even when you move on, with someone new," Deanna shouted as she walked out the door.

"Um, what?" MaryAnn's eyes grew wide. Jacob started to laugh.

"I guess we have her approval."

"I just can't." MaryAnn shook her head as she grabbed her purse. "You ready?"

"Yes, dear, I am." Joking, Jacob grabbed his keys. Stepping outside, he looked up. "Sky is getting darker. We don't have much time."

"Let's get going." MaryAnn walked over to the passenger's side of Jacob's truck, patiently waited for him to open her door and Deanna's door. He smiled as he looked at her.

MaryAnn sat, buckled herself in, and looked out the window. Jacob slid into his seat, put his hand on MaryAnn's leg, tapping it slightly. She looked over at him and smiled then returned her gaze out the window.

Oh Lord. Is it too soon? Is it too soon to want more? To want to be happy once again? Everything seems to be moving fast. Everything seems right. Seems just how it should be, just how it should have been. I just ask you, Lord, to please give me a sign, MaryAnn prayed silently.

The drive to the church did not take long. Pulling up to the donation bins, there was another person there. It was the pastor, cleaning out the bins.

"Hey, Pastor Green." Jacob opened his door.

"Jacob, my son. What brings you out?"

"I do." MaryAnn rolled her window down. "I am donating all of Eli's clothing. I still have some in the attic. I will bring them later on, when I clean it out."

"Bless your heart. I was just coming to clean this out. We have a family that just lost all their belongings in a house fire."

"Oh no. Where was that?"

"The next town over. The fire started in the basement, electrical. The Lord was with them. They were able to get everyone out including the pets. The house, though, is nothing but rubbish."

"Well, Eli would want them to have his clothes if they could fit into them."

"I do believe the father is Eli's size."

"What about the rest of the family?"

"The mother is about your size, two young girls, and an infant son."

"I will go through my clothes when we get home. I am sure I can spare some."

"I will too, Mommy."

"That's my girl. We can give them to Jacob."

"I will bring them on my way home tonight."

"Are you all sure?"

"We are, Pastor Green."

"Thank you. Jacob, just put them on the covered porch, if it's late and we are asleep."

"Will do, sir." Jacob started to grab the bags and transfer them to the pastor's truck. He looked up to see MaryAnn starting to get out. "You can sit there, Mary. I am just about done."

MaryAnn looked back and smiled. She closed her door and buckled once again. Jacob finished up, got back into the truck, and headed to the local hardware store. There they walked down the paint aisle, picking colors out for the kitchen, living room, dining room, bedrooms, hallway, and even bathroom. Jacob knew it would not all get done in a day, but that just means more weekends or days off spent with Mary and Deanna. Next, they walked down and grabbed three large construction cans for the debris. As they walked up to the cashier, someone they both knew, they chatted, telling her of their grand plan. MaryAnn didn't even have a chance to get her card out. Jacob already had his in the slot and paid for it.

"Hey, I could have gotten it." MaryAnn looked up at Jacob as he signed his name.

"I know. But I wanted to." He smiled, putting his card back into his wallet. The cashier smirked. She noticed the sparks but said nothing. "Have a great evening, Holly."

"You do the same, Jacob and MaryAnn. Deanna, have fun knocking that wall down."

"I can't wait." Deanna started to skip, catching up to her mom and Jacob. They all loaded the items in the back of Jacob's truck.

"MaryAnn, why don't you and Deanna go ahead and go through your clothes? I will start knocking the wall down to make sure there is no electrical."

"Okay, that sounds like a plan." Looking over at him, she reached her hand, grabbing his, interlocking her fingers with his. He looked down briefly, then locked his fingers around hers, leaving a smile going across his face. "Thank you for today."

"You're welcome."

The drive home did not take long. Deanna sat in the back. She noticed them holding hands but did not say anything. Oddly enough, she was okay with it; not sure if it was anything or not. Hopping out of the truck, Deanna and MaryAnn quickly went inside, carrying a can of paint along with them. Grabbing trash bags, they quickly went to work sorting through their clothes. Jacob brought one of the cans in and his toolbox, going straight to work, taking the one side of the wall down, piece by piece, placing them into the large can, trying to keep control of the mess. To his amusement, the wall started to come down, with no problems.

"Hey, I have three bags of my clothes." MaryAnn came out an hour later. "Wow, Jacob, you got the wall completely stripped down to the studs."

"I am actually shocked this wall has not fell on you guys. It was barely up. When there should have been like six nails per stud, there was two to four. I do not even know how the wall itself did not fall over. Look how flimsy it is." He pushed on the two-by-fours, and they moved.

"Leave it to Eli to not do something the right way." MaryAnn shook her head.

"Mom, I have three bags to go."

"Hey, so do I. That's a good number, kid."

"Jacob. Dang, I didn't get to help."

"Really, Dee, it wasn't hard or much. When I go to take my wall down in my place, you are coming over to help with that. It will be a bear of a job."

"Promise."

"Cross my heart!"

"Deal."

"Until then, come help me take the two-by-fours down. They are not up there good, so I need you to hold them as I remove the nails from the top."

"Okay."

Deanna went over to help Jacob out as MaryAnn started to carry the bags out to Jacob's truck, placing them in the back seat just in case the rain starts to fall. Taking a breather, reflecting on today, she touched her lips, looked at her hand. She could not help but to smile.

"Hey, what are you smiling about?" Jacob made her jump as he came out with a bag.

"You. Today. This." She pointed to the bag of clothes.

"Me, me too." He tossed the bag into the truck. "That was the last bag."

"Awesome."

"The wall is down. The container is by the garage. I showed Deanna how to tape the windows, the outlets, the ceiling."

"Okay."

"It's getting late. The storm is approaching. I want to get home before it hits and drop these bags off."

"I wish you didn't have to leave."

"Me too." He put his hands on her side and pulled her into him. "I will be back before you know it." Hugging her, he kissed her forehead before letting her go.

"Promise."

"Promise."

She watched Jacob get into his truck, back out, and drive off. A sudden tug pulled on her; she did not want him to leave. Thunder cracked, making her jump. She ran inside.

"Mom, they said it's going to be bad tonight. They said massive lightning, heavy rain."

"Well, that's never good. Why don't we get the rooms we want to paint prepped for tomorrow?"

"Okay, let's start in the living room, kitchen, and dining room since it already looks new with no wall up."

"Good idea."

A few hours passed. The storm grew stronger. They finally got the rooms prepped for the paint job, just as the power went out.

"Well, that was just pure luck. Let me get the flashlights and candles."

"Mom, don't leave me alone."

"Then come with me, Dee." They headed for the back bedroom.

The thunder roared, lightning lit the sky up. MaryAnn found the flashlight, handed it to Deanna.

"Shine the light in the drawer. I know I have matches in here to light the candles with."

Lightning struck so close their hair stood up on their arms.

"This is really bad. Stay away from the windows."

"Okay, Mom."

MaryAnn found the matches. Striking one against the edge of the box, she lit a candle. Suddenly, they heard a loud crash as the sky lit up. Their fire alarm started to pierce the air.

"Mom!" Deanna screamed in fear. MaryAnn looked down the hall. She stood in shock; this cannot be happening. She grabbed her cell phone, dialing 911, as she slammed her door shut. Grabbing blankets to block smoke coming in from the bottom of the door.

"Nine-one-one, what is your emergency?"

CHAPTER 7

House

Jacob's phone brightened up the dark room. Reaching for it, he noticed it was Mark.

"Hey, Captain, what's up?"

"Get up. Get to MaryAnn's NOW!"

"What happened?" In sheer panic, Jacob flung his legs over the edge of his bed.

"It just came over the scanner. Her house was hit by lightning. The front is on fire. She cannot get out. They are in the back room."

Jacob did not have time to think. He grabbed his shirt, threw it on. Grabbing his keys, he ran out the door. Turning the truck over, he threw his four-ways on and floored it to Mary's. Thank goodness she was only two blocks away, but it seemed like he could not get there fast enough. Pulling down her road, he can see the glow of the fire in the front of the house. The fire department has not even gotten there yet. Not even bothering to turn off his truck, he jumped out of it once he put it into park. Her neighbors were standing on their porches.

"SHE IS TRAPPED! Anyone have a ladder?" Jacob yelled.

"Yeah, I do!" Mr. Thompson yelled back. He ran to the side of his garage and grabbed the wooden stepladder, running with it over to Jacob.

"She is in the back room with that tiny window. I need to get into this room, see if I can reach her and Deanna."

"Jacob, you do not have protective gear on."

"I don't care. It will be too late by time the fire department gets here. This house is not built to code. The front is already lit up."

Jacob set up the ladder. Grabbing a rock, he broke the window, unlocked it, and slid it open. Smoke came pouring out. Giving it a second, he entered the room. Lowering close to the floor, he reached the doorway; the hall was on fire, shooting across to the hall to the small spare back room. Jacob banged on the door. He could hear the sirens wailing from the outside.

"MARY!"

"JACOB!" Mary opened the door. "My house is on fire."

"I know, let's go. The hall is on fire. We do not have time. The smoke is getting thick. Stay low. Deanna, come up here with me, get under the blanket. Let's go."

Just as they turned to head back to the front room, the whole front hall became engulfed with flames.

"What do we do?" Mary started to panic.

Scanning the area as fast as he could, he said, "There right in front of us, Deanna's room, the door was shut. Not much smoke would have gotten in there."

"Deanna's room, now."

They darted across the hall; the flames nipped at their feet. Jacob quickly opened the door and shut it behind them. Grabbing blankets, he laid them on the floor against the door.

"This fire is too hot. That door won't hold long, let alone these walls or that ceiling. Get the window open. Deanna, listen to me. You have to go out the window. It is not a long drop. You can do it. Your mom will be right behind you."

"What about you?"

"I will come out right after Mommy. Let's go, we don't have much time."

MaryAnn opened the window, Jacob lifted Deanna onto the edge, with the blanket wrapped around her, and he lowered her to the ground. Pulling the blanket back up, he wrapped it around MaryAnn, lifted her onto the window's edge.

"Who will lower you?"

"Your house is one level. It's really not that far down. Now go."

MaryAnn heard the fear in his voice. She turned around to slide down the side of the house with the assistance of Jacob. The fire started to breach the wall and door. Knowing a back draft just may happen when that fire comes through that door, he quickly climbed out the window, pushing himself off the ledge, just in the nick of time. Just as he predicted, the fire hit the air and created a fireball out the window.

"Jacob!" MaryAnn ran to him. "Are you okay?"

"Mary, I am okay. Are you?" He stood up, reaching out to her. "Deanna?"

"We are okay." Mary wrapped her arms around Jacob's waist.

Jacob wrapped one arm around Mary and the other around Dee. He guided them to the front of the house, where they stood there watching the flames rip through their home. The fire department arrived along with Mark.

"Is everyone okay?" Mark walked up to the three of them.

"We are okay," MaryAnn spoke. "My house is gone, but thanks to Jacob, we are alive."

"A house can be replaced, but you cannot," Mark spoke. "Jacob, your arm, did you get burnt?"

"I am fine."

"No, that needs to be cleaned. Go to the ambulance and get that checked." He waved at the EMT, who ran over. "He has a burn on his arm. All three of them were in the house. Check them out."

Knowing there was no sense of fighting with the captain and no sense watching your life go up in flames, they followed orders and headed for the ambulance.

"What are we going to do, Mom?" Deanna broke down into tears.

"I don't know, kid."

"Well, for starters, you can come stay with me. It's dry. I have a spare room you both can sleep in."

"Jacob, I...thank you." MaryAnn looked up into his eyes. "Deanna, we will see what the insurance says. I will have to call the mortgage people for all that information. Your father took care of all of it. See what we can do. Can we rebuild, or is it better to sell the land?"

They let the EMT check them out and bandage Jacob's arm up. They refused to go to the hospital. The fire chief walked over to them, along with Mark.

"Are you guys okay?"

"Yeah. Minor burn must have happened when I was shielding them in the hall. Their lungs are clear."

"MaryAnn, I hate to say it, but your house is a complete loss. The fire got in the walls and that is all she wrote. I am not even sure if there is anything savable in the house."

"Mary, do you have somewhere to go?" Mark asked.

"Yeah, we are going to crash at Jacob's. I will call the insurance company in the morning to see what is covered and what our options are."

"You seem very calm, oddly calm."

"Mark, after all that I have been through, this is just another hurdle. I do not know why God thought he would vacate me from my own home by fire, but he must have some kind of reason. I am alive, my daughter is alive, Jacob, my hero is okay."

"Okay, kiddo. You know where I am if you need me." Mark hugged her. "Jacob, the fire department has some hot spots to tend to, but it's basically gone. Why don't you take Mary and Dee to your house? You all need to get showers."

"What are we going to wear?" Deanna cried.

"Deanna, Mrs. Shell is already on that. She is at the store as we speak right now getting you and your mother some clothes. By time you get to Jacob's and get a shower, she will have dropped them off. Speaking of her, this is her calling. Hello, honey. Yes, everything is okay. The house is not savable. How about I give you Mary? She can give you sizes. They are heading to Jacob's. I know I agree, but that's for another day." Mark handed the phone to Mary, who went and sat in Jacob's truck along with Deanna.

"Thank you, Mark."

"Take good care of her. She has been through too much."

"I will."

"You both are like my kids, but if you hurt her, I will choose her. Do you understand me?"

Jacob looked at Mark, knowing exactly what he meant. He is giving him the father talk that most guys get from the girl's dad.

"I have been head over heels, madly in love with her for how long? If I were planning to hurt her, would I have just risked my own life going into a burning building for her? I will not hurt her. I give you my word. But nothing is going on at this point. We are just taking each day as they come."

"Good boy. Now let me get my phone, and you get them to your house."

"Yes, sir."

Mark and Jacob walked over to the truck. Jacob climbed into the driver's seat, where he found Deanna sitting in the middle, Mary sitting against the window, holding Deanna. MaryAnn handed Mark his phone and thanked him.

"Let's go to my place." Jacob pulled away from the fire. He drove the short drive. Putting the truck into park, he walked over and opened the passenger's door. He reached his hand out; MaryAnn placed her hand into his. Deanna slid out behind her mother. Jacob put his arm around her as well.

"I have two showers. Mark's wife should be here at any minute. You both should go ahead and jump in. I will get my robes for you both."

"Are you sure? I can wait."

"No, Mary. You go ahead. Now that we finally how power back on, the water should be nice and warm. I will wait for Mark's wife."

"Thank you." She reached up and gave him a kiss on the cheek.

"Let me show you the bathrooms." He opened the front door. "Down the hall. This first door is the house bathroom, one that you can use, Dee. Right here is the spare room. I have two twin beds in here. They came with the house when I bought it. I will make the beds up while you both are washing up. Right across is my room and the master's bath. Mary, you can use that one. Here, Dee. Here is a nice thick soft robe. I think I used it once. It is too hot for me. You can keep it if you like it."

"Oh, this is soft. Thank you."

"You're welcome. There is soap, shampoo, and conditioner in that bathroom too."

"Okay." Deanna left the room and headed straight for the shower.

"Here, Mary. Here is my robe. You can use it." He handed her a lightweight yet soft robe. "I will give you some privacy."

"Hey, Jacob." She reached and grabbed his hand. "Thank you for saving us, for being there."

"You're welcome, beautiful. Now go get a shower." He bent in, laid his lips onto her soft lips for a quick kiss, then stepped out, closing the door behind him.

MaryAnn turned the shower on, waiting for the warm water to kick in. She closed her eyes, rethinking of life.

"Eli, I don't know why I am wanting your approval, or thoughts, on all of this. You did not ask me for approval to have an affair. The house is gone. Honestly, I do not know what to do. Jacob, he rescued us. He is always there. Why didn't you tell me he was my mystery man from high school?"

She took a deep breath. She knew that answer just as she thought the question.

"Because I would have left you for him."

Taking a deep breath, she knew it was true. There was a slight knock on the door, pulling her from her thoughts.

"Yes?" Opening the door slightly, she peeked her face out the door.

"Hey, there are some bags of clothes on the bed for you. I put the bags for Dee in the spare room."

"Thank you."

"You're welcome. As soon as you are done, I will jump in."

"Well, let me get in and get out so you have some warm water left. We gals tend to use it up."

"Oh, I am sure you do." Jacob pulled the door closed. Walking out of the room, he could not help but smile. He walked out to the dining room where Mark and Stacy were sitting at the table.

"How is she?"

"She is in shock. I don't really think it has hit her yet."

"I am sure in the morning it will hit her hard. So much has happened to that poor girl."

"I know, Mark, but when she gets knocked down, she gets right back up, stronger, even though sometimes it takes a little bit to stand."

"How is Deanna handling it all?"

"She is trying to stay strong for her mom. So it really has not hit her either that her childhood home is gone."

"Hey, did they have insurance on the house?" Stacy asked.

"I do believe they did."

"Well, don't forget, MaryAnn still has a home to go to."

"I remember. I figure I would bring that up in the morning after we contact the insurance office."

"Do you have shift tomorrow?"

"No. Day after I start the overnight week."

"I just may switch you, depending on the situation at hand."

"Okay. Just let me know."

"No, you let me know."

"Hey." MaryAnn walked into the dining room with clean new jammies on. She placed her hand on Jacob's shoulder. "You stink. Go get your shower. We left you some warm water."

"Oh, well thank you for the water and compliment." Jacob chuckled as he stood up. "Will you two be here when I get out?"

"Probably." Mark raised his coffee cup. "I am going to get another cup."

"Help yourself. You know where everything is."

Jacob marched to the bedroom, shutting his door. He can smell her sweet aroma smell. Going into the bathroom, closing that door as well, he turned the shower on and hopped right in.

MaryAnn made herself a cup of coffee and joined Stacy and Mark at the table. Deanna came out into the dining room.

"Mom."

"Yes."

"Do you think Jacob would let me use his computer? I have a paper due tomorrow. I saved it on our account so I can pull it and print it from wherever."

"I am sure he will, but I am sure your teachers will understand with everything that happened."

"I know, but I want to turn it in any way since I can. I eventually need to get a new binder and book bag too."

"Baby girl, we are going to need to replace everything that was ours." The words came out, hitting MaryAnn hard in the stomach. Everything is gone: all her baby photos of Deanna, gone; wedding album, gone; the few things she had from her parents and grandparents, gone. Fighting the tears back, her voice cracked slightly. "We will go tomorrow and get your school supplies."

"How about, if it's okay with you, MaryAnn, I pick her up from school and take her to the supply store to get them? That way you can concentrate on getting things in order."

"That would be lovely." Looking down at her cup of coffee yet touched, MaryAnn took a deep breath. A soft hand touched hers.

"Mary, it will be okay. You have such a strong support system all around you, from Jacob to Mark and me, to the girls in the salon and more. We have you. We will help you. If you choose to rebuild, we will lay the brick, one by one. Put the wall up, one at a time." Stacy looked into Mary's teary eyes.

"I just don't understand why all this is happening. Have I not been put through enough test in life?"

"'When you go through deep waters, I will be with you. When you go through rivers of difficulty, you will not drown. When you walk through the fire of oppression, you will not be burned up; the flames will not consume you.' Isaiah 43:2 is teaching us that no matter what, the Lord is there, each thing that happens not just from us to learn from it but grow from it. You have become such a loving and caring person, but with strength. When he cheated, that was the devil working through Eli. Why? Because he was weak. He has been trying to knock you down too, with all that has been happening, but you will not let him. You are defeating his attempts."

"Mark, why are you a captain? You should really be a minister."

"At one point in my life, before I knew your family, I was on a different path. I had a tragic incident that brought me to the Lord and to your parents. Ever since then, I have relied on my faith, on the Bible's teachings so that one day I could help someone else out, like you."

"Hey." Jacob walked back out into the kitchen.

"Jacob, can I use your computer? I need to finish my paper that is due tomorrow."

"Sure, kiddo. Let me turn it on." He guided Deanna to the computer room. "If you need to print it, you can do that as well."

"Jacob, can I ask you something?"

"Anything."

"Do you care about my mom?"

"I care about her and you."

"No, I mean, do you really care about my mom? Do you love my mom?"

"Yes, yes, I do. But you do not have to worry. We are just friends. Your father was my best friend."

"So?"

"So it's like a code. You don't date or marry your friend's spouse."

"Dad is dead. I am sure he would not mind. I know my mom shares the same feelings."

"How do you know that?"

"You can tell by the way she looks at you."

"Well, as happy as that makes me feel, the code is enforced even when one is dead."

"The code is silly, if you ask me. I've never seen my mom look at my dad the way she looks at you. I think you two would be super silly not to date."

"You would be okay having me in your life in that way?"

"Well, you have always been there. So it is nothing new. Knowing you are there forever would be even better."

"Well, I am here forever."

"What if some girl comes and sweeps you off your feet and marries you? You have your own children, then you will not be here like you are now."

"First off, why are you talking so grown?"

"Mommy raised me this way, I guess."

"Second off, that won't happen. I tried to date other women, but it doesn't work."

"Because they are not my mom."

"Ugh, Dee, you're killing me."

"Kill the code." Deanna smiled as she sat at the desk.

Jacob shook his head as he headed for the door, only to find Mark standing outside the room.

"She has a point."

"Really, Mark?"

"Yep. She has a great point. For such a young age, she is much smarter than you."

"Let's just take each day as it comes."

"Stacy and I, we are heading out. Call if you need anything, I mean it. A week off, to be with them, anything."

"I can't afford a week off."

"I didn't say not paid. We have other things we could do to make sure you get paid."

"I will let you know tomorrow."

"Good answer. Take it easy."

Jacob and MaryAnn walked Stacy and Mark out the door. They stood there as they pulled out of the driveway. Stepping aside, he walked over to the couch and sat down. MaryAnn closed the door and locked it.

"What are you watching?"

"Most likely a movie of some sort. I can't fall asleep just yet."

"Do you mind if I join you?"

"No, Mary, I would love it if you joined me." Jacob scooted over a little.

MaryAnn sat next to Jacob, leaning into him. He wrapped his arms around her, holding her tightly. She shivered a little, so he grabbed the blanket from the back of the couch, laying it over her. They said nothing; they did not have to. The comfort they both felt in each other's arms soothed them, easing all worries away. An hour passed; Deanna finally emerged from the office. She walked into the living room to see her mother in Jacob's arms. They were both fast asleep. Moving softly, not to disturb them, she grabbed the second blanket from the love seat and laid it over Jacob, letting them sleep in each other's arms. Tiptoeing to the spare room, she knelt down on her knees beside the bed and prayed.

"Lord, I know you can hear me. I do not know why you chose to take my father from us, nor do I know why you let the house become destroyed in flames. One day, fill me in, okay? Lord, I am not praying for me. I am praying for my mother. She may be strong, but anymore tosses at her just might break her. She is the strongest person I have ever known. Lord, I see the love that Jacob has for my mother and the love my mother has for him, but is it too soon? Will they ever drop the 'code'? My mom deserves happiness, something I have not seen in her in an exceptionally long time, even before Daddy died, and now, I know the truth and I know why. Lord, why did you not protect Daddy from the devil? I wish I could hear your answers, Lord. I truly do."

She got up, crawled into bed, and fell fast asleep.

The morning sun peeked through the curtains, hitting Jacob right in the eyes. When he could not move his arms to rub his eyes, he noticed she was still there in his arms, asleep. The TV was still on; they had fallen asleep in each other's arms. MaryAnn started to stir. Her eyes fluttered opened.

"Good morning, beautiful," Jacob softly spoke.

"I cannot believe I fell asleep."

"With all that has happened, I can. I just remember covering you. I don't remember covering me." Jacob was puzzled.

"That's because I did." Deanna walked out into the living room. "You looked cold and you two looked comfy. So I covered you and went to bed. Mom, my friend Alice and her mother are going to pick me up for school. I want to go."

"Okay. You want to go, so you should. Don't forget Stacy said she wants to pick you up and take you shopping, but mind your manners. Don't overspend."

"I know, Mom. I know."

"I am going to get up and call the insurance company, get things rolling with the house."

"Okay. But, Mom, we are okay here with Jacob until the meantime. That bed was super comfy."

"Get to school, silly girl."

"Have an awesome day, Dee. If you decide at any point it is too much to be there, call me. I will come get you."

"Thanks, Jacob, but I will be just fine." Deanna smiled as she headed for the front door. "Should I have Stacy bring me here when we are done?"

"Yes. There is a spare key hanging up by the door. Grab that just in case we are not here." Jacob pointed to the key rack.

"Okay." Deanna walked out of the house to her friend's car.

"She is strong, just like you, Mary."

"I think she might be stronger to be honest."

"Doubtful. You have been tested way too much."

"Well, I guess I should start calling the insurance company. They can look the policy up by name or social, right? All the papers in the kitchen are gone."

"Yes, they have ways to find your information. You go ahead, and I will cook us some breakfast, eggs, toast, and bacon. Sound good?"

"Sounds perfect." MaryAnn got up from the couch, out from the warmth of his arms and the blanket. She grabbed her cellphone, looked up under her contacts, her insurance company. Jacob went to work in the kitchen.

"Ultra-Insurance Company, how may assist your call?"

"Hi. Yes, my name is MaryAnn Baker. My house was hit by lightning last night and burned to the ground. What do I do?"

"I am so sorry to hear about that, Mrs. Baker. Let's first pull up your information."

MaryAnn gave her her phone number, house address, her social, and Eli's social security number.

"Okay, Mrs. Baker. It looks like your late husband adjusted the insurance. He took it down to the bare minimal needed for the mortgage."

"What does that mean?"

"Meaning, it does not cover fire, electrical, nothing. He kept the flood insurance only because you're in a flood zone, which was enough to keep the mortgage people happy."

"So you're telling me, I have no way to rebuild? I have no coverage unless we flooded out? How much did that save him?"

"It looks like your insurance went down almost one hundred dollars monthly, started about four months or so ago."

"That bastard." MaryAnn broke into angry tears. "I'm sorry. Why would he do that?"

"Mrs. Baker, I am terribly sorry. We can't help you with this matter."

MaryAnn hung the phone up and sat on her bed. Putting her hands into her face, she started to cry.

Eli, you bastard. I cannot believe you did that. What were you doing with that money? Were you spending that on your affair? Eli, you have hurt me for the last and final time. Lord, no more tests. I cannot handle it.

Jacob walked in the room, seeing MaryAnn sitting on the bed with her face in her hands, rocking back and forth, praying, talking.

"Mary." Jacob walked over to her, putting his hand on her shoulder. "Mary, what happened?"

"He canceled the insurance. Kept the flood insurance because he had to but canceled the rest. I have nothing to rebuild with."

"Wait, what?"

"Saved him close to one hundred dollars a month. He did it around the time he started his affair."

"Mary, I just don't know what to say. I can't believe he did that to, not just you, but Deanna too."

"Jacob, I have no home, no place to go to."

"Mary, you can stay here for as long as you need to, want to."

"Jacob, thank you, but we can't intrude. You are too kind…"

"But you need your own home, space. I understand."

"And right now, I am homeless. I am going to have to sell the property off to pay off the mortgage. Hopefully that will leave enough down deposit too."

"Mary, you're not homeless."

"Jacob...this is your home."

"I am not talking about this place."

MaryAnn looked at him, not understanding where he was going with this.

"Mary, you have a home to return to. You just have to push through the past."

It dawned on her; he was talking about her home, her family home, the house that sits, trapped in time, the house that has not been lived in for so long, the house that she grew up in that holds the memories of her parents.

"How do you know about that house?" Her tears of anger switched to pure pain.

"Mark, he has us patrol it. Lately I have been doing the inside check, run the water, make sure everything is ready for your return."

"Why didn't you tell me you...you knew?"

"It's not my past to tell."

"I don't think I could bring myself to step inside the house."

"You can, you will, and I will be there with you. Mary, darling, you never had closure from that day. That is why you did not recognize me the day Eli introduced you to me. That is why life keeps repeating things. We need to get closure for you. Remember John 14:27: 'I am leaving you with a gift-peace of mind and heart. And the peace I give is a gift the world cannot give.' So don't be troubled or afraid. The house being struck by lighting is the closing of your and Eli's chapter, but the closing of your parent's chapter begins the day you step one foot in your childhood home, a gift that you can do."

"Is there anything else you know?"

"Nope. Now you know all my secrets. You know that my heart belongs to you when you are ready, you know I am forever here, no matter what you choose, and you know I will not let you go in the house alone, that I will be there every single step. What you do not know is breakfast is getting cold, that it is done. So let's go eat."

MaryAnn chuckled as she looked up into his eyes. She reached out to his hands. Standing up, she looked into his eyes.

"Just know, I love you too, but I need time to process all that has happened."

"Take all the time in the world." He bent down and planted his lips onto hers, but only for a split second. "Come, let's go eat. Then we will go see your home."

"Okay."

They walked out to the kitchen. Just as they finished saying grace, there was a knock on the door.

"I wonder who that would be." Jacob stood up and headed to the door. Opening, standing there was Mark. "Hey, Cap, everything okay?"

"Yep, just checking on Mary and making sure you behaved yourself last night."

Jacob shook his head. "Yes, I was a good boy. Do you want some breakfast?"

"No, thanks." Mark followed Jacob to the dining room. "Hey, Mary, how's it going?"

"Well, found out that, one, Eli canceled our home insurance, kept the flood only to save him money to spend on his girlfriend, and two, that you and Jacob knew about my childhood home."

"Eli did what now?"

"Yeah, I have no insurance to fix the house, nothing covered, unless there was a flood."

"How the heck was that possible with having mortgage?"

"Some loophole they found."

"Mary, I am so sorry to hear that. What are you going to do?"

"Well, my plan is to sell the land. Jacob is going to go with me to my childhood home. I need to close that chapter in my life in order to move forward."

"Good, your house, it has been patiently waiting for you."

"Thank you, Mark, for taking care of it. I honestly did not know you were until Jacob mentioned it."

"It's paid off, the taxes are up to date, the heat has been on, the air conditioner has been ran. It is like someone has been living there the whole time, but it has been vacant. Stacy and I, we go in a clean it once a week, detail clean once a month to keep the dust down. We did not move a thing. Everything is just as it was when your grandparents locked the door."

"It is?"

"Yes."

"Jacob, I would like to go now."

"Really?"

"Yes."

"Okay, why don't you go get dressed? We will head right over."

MaryAnn got up, walked to the spare room, and shut the door.

"Jacob, you have the next week off, paid. Just take care of MaryAnn. Get that property cleaned up and listed or start the process. She needs to call her car insurance as well. The fire started back up after you left and hot timbers hit her car. Let's just say it is not fixable. The fire department did their best with what they could, with the wind and whatnot. I don't know what Eli was thinking when he put so much hot flammable, cheap insulation into that home when he remodeled it. Then again, I don't know what he was thinking when he dropped his coverage on his home to cover up his affair."

"He was my very best friend, a player in high school. But never in my mind did I think he would stoop so low." Jacob shook his head. "He was like another person, someone I didn't even know."

"I agree. He was not raised that way. I can tell you that for sure, so I just do not know where he got it from."

"Thanks for getting me the week off. MaryAnn is going to need all the support she can get at the moment."

"Let me know if there is anything more that we can do."

"You have done plenty." MaryAnn walked from the back room.

"Well, since you're out, let me break some more bad news. The fire restarted, and well, let's say it as it is: you need a new car. Hot timbers hit it and it is not fixable."

"Well, at least I know I have insurance on that, just not sure what kind."

"The firemen are doing the boot pass for you."

"What is that?"

"They send the boot around their department, neighboring departments and town to help raise money to help you out."

"Oh, no. That is okay. Tell them to donate it to someone who really could use it."

108

"MaryAnn, I told them you would say that, and they all agree it belongs to you once it is filled."

"Well, let's not argue over it now. There is a house to be seen." Jacob stood up, grabbing his keys. "Mary, you can call the car insurance from the car."

"Now that sounds like a plan," Mark rejoiced.

"Okay, this argument is on hold for now." MaryAnn looked at Mark. "Jacob, let's go before I change my mind."

MaryAnn marched to the front door and headed for Jacob's truck. Running to catch up with her, he grabbed the passenger's door before she had the chance to open in it.

"When will you ever learn that a gentleman is supposed to open the door for a lady, house, car, whatever door?"

"And when will you learn that yes, that is so very nice for you to do that this lady has not had that nice gesture in so long it will take some time to get used to?"

"Okay, you are right." Smirking, he opened the door. "There ya go, my lady."

"Well, thank you, sir." With a giggle, MaryAnn climbed into the truck. She watched Jacob walk in a fast past to the driver's side.

"Are you ready for this?" He started the truck, putting into reverse.

"Honestly, I am kind of nervous."

"That is to be expected." Putting the truck into drive, he reached for her hand. "But that is why I am here: to be there for you. Why don't you go ahead and call the car insurance place?"

"Okay." Taking the opposite hand, she searched in her contacts for the number. Jacob looked over at her, surprised she did not let go of his hand.

"Hi, yes, I need to call to report a fire to my car. No, no, it was caused by my house. My house caught on fire due to lightning and then sparked a blaze on my car in the driveway."

Jacob kept driving, listening to her conversation. So many questions they were asking her; it was frustrating him. It is very simple: her house is destroyed and now is her car. Her life was flipped over several times over.

"Ugh, that is what I figured. I do not know about the second car. We do not have one, that must be a mistake. Yes, you can cancel that. No, no, I know it was not you but just how everything seems to be going. Okay. That is fine. So you will handle all of that? My email is on file. Can you send me a confirmation of all of that? Okay, thank you. You have a great day as well."

"Well, that did not sound well."

"Nope, it was not." Mary started to shake her head. "But you know what? It helps close the chapter of Eli completely. He lowered our insurance to the bare minimum needed for the loan. Since this was a buy-here pay-here type loan through the dealership, we didn't need full coverage. But he had full coverage on another car. We don't have another car."

"You don't think…?"

"Would he?"

"At this point, I don't even think I knew my best friend."

"Well, if he did, she no longer has it, and you know what? I could care less. I wonder, if he did, would the car be in his name as well?"

"I would think so. We will have to run his DL number. After we are done with the house, we can run to the station and we can do that."

"Let's because if there is another car out there in his name, it belongs to me. I rather give it to someone else."

"Mary…"

"I know, Jacob, it is not the Christian thing to do, but he broke the vow, not me."

"No, I was going to say, it's your car. Do what you want, but we are here." He pulled into the driveway. Still holding her hand, she squeezed his just a little tighter.

"I don't know if I can do this."

"You can and you will." Jacob got out of the truck and walked over to her door, opening it for her. He reached his hand out to hers. "I will be here every single step of the way. Come, my love, let's go in."

She looked into his eyes; she liked hearing him say those words. She gripped his hand as she got out of the truck. He held on to her hand as they walked to the front door. Taking the key out, unlocking the door, and pushing it open, MaryAnn closed her eyes. The scents hit her. She smelled her mother, her father, the house. Taking a deep breath, she walked in, still holding Jacob's hand, tightly.

"You have this," Jacob whispered as he followed her into the house.

"It's like…it's like it's stuck in time." MaryAnn could not believe what she was seeing. Her childhood home, frozen in time. "That chair right there, that used to be my dad's favorite spot. He would sit there, he would read us the Bible, sing songs. Over there, Mommy loved that spot. She would sit there and make things, knit, or crochet, whichever was easier for the pattern she was working on."

Touching the knickknacks on the shelf, tears began to fall. Taking a deep breath, she headed for the kitchen.

"Mommy used to bake and make so much in this kitchen as she homeschooled me. Neither one of them wanted me in public school, but because I begged and I begged and kept my grades up, they put me into the high school. They said God gave them a sign that they should allow me to go on this journey. I guess he knew he was going to be calling them home on that very day."

"And it was not your time just yet."

"Jacob, what am I going to do with this house?"

"What do you mean?"

"This is the house of my childhood, this is my parent's house, this house holds so many amazing memories, but one horrific day, one horrific memory darkens this house."

"Do you want to sell it?"

"No, I could never sell it."

"Do you want to live in it?"

"Yes, but no."

"Why don't you renovate the house? Make it new, make it you."

"I don't know if that would be right."

"Look, I didn't get to really meet your parents, but most parents, when they leave the homestead to the children, they expect them to renovate, make it their family home. I can help you. We can take it slow, go through things, keep things you truly want to keep, and donate the rest. For the stories I hear told, your parents were always trying to help others out."

"You are right about that. They always were reaching their arms out to help folks in need. They would want me to be happy. I just wish I got to tell them about you. I came home that day ready to brag about you. Tell my mom, I made some new friends and one friend helped me feel safe in the school, helped me. That was you."

"Well, let's go into the living room, sit where you would have sat. Put a photo in each of their chairs and have that moment. Just close your eyes. Although they are not here physically, they are here spiritually. They will hear you, they will listen, and if you listen, you too will hear them. If you want, I will leave the house."

"No, Jacob, please stay. Knowing you're still here will make me feel more comfortable."

"Okay, let's go talk to your mom and dad." Looking into her eyes, he led her into the living room. "Where would you have sat?"

"Right there in the middle."

"Okay." He walked her over to that very spot. Letting her sit, he grabbed a family photo from the table and placed it on her dad's chair then grabbed another photo and placed it where her mother sat.

"Jacob, I don't know how to start." Looking up at him, she felt a little silly.

"Just start talking like it was that day, first day of high school. Whatever memory you blocked out, I am sure once you get going, it will all come flooding back. I am going to sit right there in the doorway. The room is yours."

Silence filled the air. MaryAnn was not too sure how to talk to her parents with him here, but she did not want him to leave. She felt her chest feel heavy, like it was filling up with air. The warm sensation ran through her body, and just like that, the sense of smell, her parents were there.

"Mom, Dad, I truly do not know how to begin. That day, you were taken from me, changed my life completely. That day, I came home, I ran through that door, looking for you. I wanted to tell you just how nervous I was, first time ever in school and I was a freshman in high school. I wanted to tell you how awesome that day was. I met some new friends. They were excited to show me the ropes, then a boy, he bumped into me but helped me to pick up my books that I dropped. He even talked to me. His blue eyes, he was very kind. Even when we passed on our way through the cafeteria, he asked me how my day was going. I wanted to tell him it was better, thanks to him. I did not get his name, and I know you would have said, 'That is okay, just reintroduce yourself to him.' Dad, you would have said, 'Stay away from the boys.' But, Dad, there was something totally different about him. I wanted to tell you, Mom, that all the teaching you did, they were considering putting me up a grade or two because I was truly ahead the class, with the test they had me do in the summer. I want to tell you thank you for letting me go, that I love you two so much and I really did miss you, and I miss you guys sooo much right now. So much has happened. I found that boy, years later, but I married his best friend, and well, you know all this because you are here, you have seen the good, the bad, and the ugly. That boy, his name is Jacob, and he is truly the best, best friend I could have ever asked for. And maybe one day it will feel right to court him, but I really don't know since I am a widow to his best friend, that neither one of us truly knew. This is all the stuff I would be talking to you about, Mom, asking for you great advice, but I am not getting the answers anymore." She remembered what Jacob said: listen, they may talk back. "I am thinking of moving back into the homestead since well, my house burned down, and it was not covered with insurance, but if it's okay with you, I think I want to renovate it: new kitchen, new living room, but that is only if it's okay with you. Just wish I can hear your answers."

MaryAnn looked up at Jacob, sitting there quietly. Wiping her tears from her face, she stood up and walked over to him.

"I just wish I could hear their voice."

"I know."

"I just want to know if they would be okay with me changing the house."

"I am sure they will be." Jacob got up, grabbing the chair to put back into the kitchen. As he swung the chair around, it very so slightly hit the wall, but just enough that a photo fell off the wall, taking wallpaper with it. "Well, I think you got your answer right there."

Standing there in disbelief, MaryAnn grabbed the photo. It was a photo of just her parents holding each other, smiling, happy, in love, and she was pregnant with her.

"I got a few answers." The feeling of calm sensation crossed over her. "Let's lock up, go to the station. I want to give her the option of putting the car into her name and insurance or she can turn it over to me. Then I want to get some donation boxes and bring Deanna here, with her and you. I want to come up with a game plan for the house. Then I need to go see the bank to see if I can get a construction loan to do renovations to this place, hire someone to get it done, and don't say you can do it because we both know you have to return to work next week and this project will take longer than that."

"Who are you?"

"Don't pick on me. I am the girl you are in love with, the girl that is still working out some issues, but the girl that loves you back." She turned, looking into his eyes. "I fell in love with you the day you bumped into my arm in the hall. I was lost but still madly in love with you when I fell in love with Eli and married him. I wish I didn't block out that day so I would realize sooner who you were. I would have left Eli then for you. Deanna would have been ours."

"Let's not live on what ifs and 'I wish I would have.'" He put his hands on her hips, bringing her closer. "Let's live for today."

"Okay, let us live for today but take each day at a time. I don't want to rush into things."

"My love, take all the time you need. I am not going anywhere." His hands moved from her hips, slowly went on each side of her cheeks, bringing her lips to his, taking his breath away as they touched.

MaryAnn wrapped her arms around his neck, running her fingers through his hair, kissing his lips back. This time, the kiss did not last just for seconds; it lasted for minutes—minutes that felt like hours. Holding her tightly, Jacob knew this was it, no turning back; this is what he has been long waiting for.

"Let's go dig up some dirt." MaryAnn smiled. "Jacob, let's keep us to ourselves for a little."

"Okay."

"I just don't want the questions and the pressure from everyone else. I really just want to take our time."

"Okay. I can handle that." He kissed her on the forehead. "Shall we head to the station?"

"We shall." MaryAnn placed her hand into his hand. "Thank you, thank you for doing everything and bringing me home. Thank you for thinking of the idea of talking to my parents. I would have never thought of that."

"Mary, you do not have to thank me. It is an honor to do it for you." He stroked her cheek and walked out the front door.

The drive to the station seemed to be very peaceful, still hand in hand, fingers interlocked together. He parked near the front door.

"Are you ready for the locals, the 'I'm sorry to hear about the fire'? Or is there anything we can do for you?"

"Ugh, can you just put me in your pocket and take me to your desk?"

"Ha! I wish I could keep you all to myself." Smirking, Jacob got out of the truck. He walked over and opened Mary's door. "Come on, my dear. Let us face the fire line and find out the info that we already know."

"Let's." MaryAnn took his hand and got out of the truck. They walked through the doors, and just as he said, the sympathy lines started.

"MaryAnn." Officer Becky Smith looked up from the front desk. "I am terribly sorry to hear about your home. If there is anything I can do for you? Please let me know."

"Thanks, Becky, I appreciate it."

"How are you, Serg?" Becky batted her eyes, making MaryAnn giggle.

"Well, I am off duty but need my desk for a matter in hand. So if anyone calls for me, I am still not here."

"Yes, sir."

Jacob pulled on Mary's hand as they walked up the steps. Still giggling, she took a deep breath and followed him.

"Man, she has it bad for you."

"Not my type." He shook his head with annoyance. "She does that all the time and it drives me crazy. She knows I am really not interested."

"Some just don't understand that until you're officially off the market." She continued to follow him in a quick pace, avoiding any and all other encounters. Finally, they walked into an office. "Jacob, you actually have an office?"

"Well, when your second-in-command under the captain, of course you do, but I am barely in here unless it's for a civilian appointment or do my monthly paperwork. I'd rather be out in the public taking care of things."

"That's what makes you amazing, liked and well trusted."

"Okay, so let's look it up. Do you happen to know his DL?"

"I actually do. I needed it for all the papers after he died. Here, it's saved in my phone." She pulled up the notes in her phone. "Here it is." Showing him the driver's license number, Jacob started to type away.

"I heard you two were in here." Captain Shell walked in the room.

"Hey, Mark." MaryAnn looked up. "The house, it's just as it was. Thank you so much." She got up from Jacob's side and walked over to give him a hug.

"Oh, you sweet girl, it was my pleasure. So what brought you in?"

"Along with his affair, Eli got another car. He took the full coverage off Mary's since the payments are just about complete, leaving it with bare minimal coverage."

"Let me guess, your car is not covered, and he put full coverage on another car?"

"Yes, I told the lady I talked to we didn't have another car, and she insisted that he did. I had her remove the car from the insurance, something she has to get authorization on since it shows he has another car registered to him."

"So you're here to find that car."

"Yep. We are not breaking any laws because technically it's my car if it's in his name."

"What are you going to do when you find it?"

"I don't know yet."

"'Then you will know the truth, and the truth will set you free' [John 8:32]," Mark spoke. "Just remember Proverbs 29:11 when Jacob takes you to the car: 'Fools give full vent to their rage, but the wise bring calm to the end.' Pray as you head into the direction you are about to go."

"You always give the simplest answers, full of wise, inspiring phrases or verses."

"I lean on the Lord. He has me as he has you and as soon as you start to understand that life will start to make sense again, for the both of you."

"Mary, I have it. He does have another car registered. It has a loan on it."

"When did he get it?"

"Do you really want to know?"

"Yes."

"Mary, he got it two days before his accident."

"What?"

"Yep. There is an address too, and it is not yours."

"So you're telling me, he was still seeing her, even after I found out, even after we were trying to fix things?"

"That's what it looks like."

"Mark, can I divorce a corpse?" Mary started to shake her head.

"No, you can't, but what you can do is go to her, hear her side of the story. Yes, even after what she said at the funeral. You have to make amends, just as you did with your parents' house. You cannot close chapters without getting closure in them. Go. Take care of business. Jacob, you have to be the monitor."

"Yes, sir," they both said at the same time.

Jacob stood, with the printed information in hand. He walked over to Mary and took her hand.

"Come, Mary, let's go close this chapter. Once this chapter is closed, then we can start a new one."

"Let me know how you two make out."

"Will do, Cap," Jacob replied as they walked out the door. Again, avoiding as many people as they could, they snuck out the back door, walking in quick pace to the truck.

"Are you ready for this?"

"As long as you're by my side, Jacob, I can accomplish anything that comes my way."

"Forever by your side, I will be." Jacob started the truck. They headed south, just outside of town, to a housing development. The ride was filled with silence. MaryAnn just kept looking out the window, saying a silent prayer. The drive did not take too long. After twenty minutes, Jacob pulled off the highway. Making a right onto the first road, he pulled up to a new developed house. Sitting in the driveway was a newer sedan.

"I am really hoping she had this house before their affair started."

"In a way, so am I. But to be honest, I really don't know anymore." Jacob took a deep breath. Something is telling him; this house was bought with Eli.

"Well, it's now or never." MaryAnn did not give Jacob the moment to open her door. She quickly opened her door and slid out of the truck. Jacob did not say a single word. He just followed MaryAnn up the pathway. She took a deep breath and rang the doorbell.

Tabby answered the door. "We need to talk."

"MaryAnn? Jacob? What are you two doing here? How did you find me?"

"Your car is in my husband's name."

"So you have come to take it?"

"No, I came to find out the truth."

"Tabby, may we come in?" Jacob spoke up, not wanting to do this outside in the public eye, not sure if tempers were going to flare up.

"If you truly must." Tabby seemed nervous.

"Or we can stand in the chilly air." MaryAnn looked at her.

"Come in." Tabby opened the door. "We can sit in the kitchen. Can I offer you any tea?"

"No, no, thank you," MaryAnn replied, calmly. She noticed that Tabby was trying to avoid the living room at all cost. They sat at the table.

"What do you want to know?"

"Everything. The details minus the bedroom talk. I need to close this chapter, but I need the truth. Who came onto to whom?"

"He...he came onto me. MaryAnn, I know it was wrong. I knew he was married. Then he lied to me, just as he lied to you. He told me that you two were on the verge of a separation that is going to lead to a divorce. He told me he was unhappy and has been for so long. Then he started to tell me sweet things. So one thing led to another. One thing led to a lunch date then to dinner dates. The way he was in public made me believe that you two really were breaking up. He told me that you were keeping the house, that he wanted to take our relationship up to the next level. So we bought this house together. We were talking about the future. He said when he would ask me to marry him, he wanted it to be special. He wanted to have children. He wanted Deanna to be a big sister and to one day, hopefully, for her to join us as a family. When he told you he stopped seeing me, he was still coming over. He told me he had to tell you this, he had to pretend to work things out because the lawyer suggested it. He said he hated lying to you, Jacob, you were his guy, his best friend, but he knew how much MaryAnn meant to you and knew things would be different between you two. He believed in his heart that in the end you would understand. But when I saw you and how you acted at his service, I realized that he lied to me as much as he lied to you, MaryAnn, and I am so sorry. I was so stupid. I know you just lost your house and your car in the fire. You have every right to this home and car. I just ask that you give me some time to find a place to live and a new sedan."

"Wow. That was a lot to take in. A lot all in one shot. To be honest, I feel sorry for you. I am no longer angry at you. He fooled you just as he fooled me. Is there anything else I need to know?" MaryAnn knew something else was not right.

Tabby took a deep breath and stood up from the table, pushing her oversized shirt close to her belly.

"I am due in four more months." Her little baby bump poked out.

Jacob quickly looked at MaryAnn, expecting her to flip out. But to his astonishment, she did not. She took a deep breath.

"Mary, are you okay?" he asked in concern.

"Yes, my love, I am. 'Likewise, you who are younger, be subject to elders. Clothe yourselves, all of you with humility toward one another, for "God opposes the proud but gives grace to the humble"' [1 Peter 5:5]. My mother used to say that verse to me and now I know why. Tabby, I cannot promise that we will be best friends, I cannot promise that at all. It's only in the future that time will tell. But what I can promise you: this is grace. No, I am not taking the car, but you need to take it and change it into your name. No, I am not taking the house, that too needs to be put into your name. I will give you six months to figure the house out, but I need the car out of his name ASAP so I can get myself a non-burnt one. I will tell Deanna about the baby and leave it up to her if she wants to contact you and see the baby when it is born if you want. One thing I do want to tell you is I am sorry. I am sorry he allowed the devil to take over and bring you in. I pray that one day you find your prince charming that you deserve. I pray that you have God in your heart."

"MaryAnn, I do not know what to say. You are being so kind to me, and I do not deserve it. Thank you."

"You're welcome."

"I would love for Deanna to see her sister, when she is born, that is only if she wants to."

"It's a girl?"

"Yes. Not sure on the name though. I just don't know."

"Hope," MaryAnn spoke. "For she is your hope. Hope to a brighter future. Hope for things to turn out for you."

"Hope." Tabby looked at Jacob. "Hope, I like it."

"I think we best get going. We need to meet Dee at your house soon." MaryAnn stood up. Even though she was being kind, nice, she was about to break. Jacob stood next to her.

"MaryAnn, thank you for everything. I am so sorry for everything. I will take care of the car and house ASAP. I will be making a call to my lawyer to work on it."

"If you need a letter of payments being made, I will write that up. You can reach me at the salon or just leave a message there for me."

"Okay, thank you." Tabby followed them down the hall. She watched as Mary paused and looked in the living room. On the wall were photos of Tabby and Eli. Ultrasound photos. Photos of him kissing her belly. So he knew.

MaryAnn took a deep breath. Jacob noticed her breathing pattern has changed and he quickly placed his hand on her hip and led her out the front door. Not saying another word, he led her to the truck, opening her door. She slid in. She held it together until they hit the highway.

"JACOB, HOW COULD HE! He bought a house with her. He bought her a car. He was still with her after we were working on our marriage. He told her we were getting a divorce. He fathered a baby with her. I did not even know my own husband. He was living two lives, two completely different lives. How am I going to break this to Deanna? He was her world. Jacob, what am I going to do?"

"You will breathe. You will get through this, just as you have gotten through so much more in your life."

"Take me to his grave." Mary looked over at Jacob.

"Are you sure?" Shocked, Jacob questioned her.

"Take me there please." She was sure.

Jacob did just as she asked. They drove the twenty minutes, in complete silence, back into town and headed straight for the graveyard. They came to a stop.

"Stay here. Please." She got out of the truck. She walked over to Eli's spot of rest. Anger filled her. She looked at his headstone. "Eli Baker. Loving Husband, Father, and Friend." "This is not true, not one bit. Eli, you really were not a loving father nor husband. You were a fake, phony, cheater. You were not even a good friend. If you were that unhappy, why stay married? For face?" MaryAnn took a deep breath, keeping her tears back. "Well, let me ask you one question: How do you like the place you are in? How do you like hell with Satan? You decided to follow him the day you decided to cheat on your wife, me, and father another baby with the other woman.

Guess what, Eli? I will no longer morn you. I will no longer be sad you're gone. I am no longer crushed. God tells us to forgive even the weakest of the weak. So I forgive you. I know when I go, I will not have to see you. God is in my heart. You know, Eli, I just do not understand, and I will never understand. I do understand that the love you never truly gave me, there is someone who will, whom has, and in time, will get the chance to, a chance to be more of man that you have ever been. So goodbye, Eli. Goodbye forever."

As MaryAnn turned around, she knew this would be the last time she would ever visit his grave site. The man she never truly knew. Taking a deep breath, she opened her door.

"I am going to deed my plot over to Tabby. She can lie next to him." She slid into the passenger's side of the truck.

"What?"

"When my day is up, put me somewhere else. This chapter, the chapter of Eli, in my book of life is closed and closed forever. Sealed."

"Mary, you're just really hurt right now. Make that decision when you're aware of it."

"Jacob, I don't even know who my so-called husband truly was. Did he at any point love me completely, honestly? Was I just a trophy on his wall? Did he have to marry me, for face, because his parents were not going to deed the dealership over to him? I know about that, Jacob. His parents thought he was not responsible enough."

"Mary, I like to think he at one point loved you more than life itself. I like to believe he did not marry you just to get the business, but I also would like to believe he would have never done any of this."

"But he did. Maybe at one point he loved me, but I honestly believe it was to get the business more so. Maybe I was not his true love, maybe Tabby is. The life he built with her seemed a lot more meaningful than the one he had with me."

"Then why not come clean? Why not tell you, divorce you?"

"For face." She took a deep breath. "Tabby will get the deed in the mail once I finish the paperwork. Do you think Charlie will help me get into another car?"

"We can ask him. Would you like to head over there?"

"Yes, I need a car. I need to start rebuilding my life, not just for myself, but for my daughter too. We need to start over, I need to hire a contractor, I want to remodel my home before we move in. I need to get back to the salon and just start living. I need to go to the funeral home office and get that plot deeded over to her. So much to do and I cannot keep asking you to take off from the station and use your time on me. It is not fair to you."

"MaryAnn, you do not need to worry about my time." He looked over into her eyes. "Let me worry about my time. I'd rather be there by your side helping you as much as I can."

"Jacob—"

"Mary." Jacob smirked as he cut her off. "To the dealership we go."

"Thank you." She reached and grabbed his hand. "I am glad I have you."

Peering out her window, she closed her eyes. Finally, after many of months of feeling empty, lost, she felt purpose. MaryAnn felt peace. What more can hit her?

CHAPTER 8

Secrets Exposed

They pulled into the dealership lot. The few salesmen outside just stared as they spotted MaryAnn.

"Why are they just glaring?"

"I have no clue. Maybe they know about everything that is going on and are surprised to see you here?"

As they pulled up to a parking spot, Charlie (he owned the dealership with Eli's father. When his father died, it was left for Charlie to own along with Eli) stepped out the door. MaryAnn just glanced over at Jacob. He shrugged his shoulders.

"I have no clue, Mary." Putting his truck into park, he opened his door.

"Hey there, Jacob. What brought you two down?" Charlie walked over, shaking Jacob's hand.

"Hey there, Charlie." Returning the shake, he let go. "Mary needs a new car. She lost her car in the house fire."

Charlie watched Jacob walk around the truck to open the passenger's door for MaryAnn.

"Hey there, MaryAnn."

"Hey, Charlie." Walking around the truck, she reached her hand out to shake his hand. Instead, he brought her in for a hug.

"How are you doing, kid?"

"I am okay. Just taking one day at a time."

"I am sure." Charlie let go of MaryAnn. "So you finally come down to see me?"

"Well, I need to talk to you about trying to replace my car I lost in the fire."

"Okay, we can get you into something. Let's go into my office. I need to show you something now that you are here."

"Your office?" MaryAnn stopped dead walking.

"My office, Eli's office, is exactly how it was left the day he left here. Nobody has gone in there."

"Oh. Is that why you were calling me, asking me to come down?"

"No, MaryAnn. I need to go over some paperwork."

"Oh." MaryAnn did not understand "paperwork." She signed all the documents she thought she would need to for his work. She followed Charlie into the dealership, with Jacob right behind her. Everyone stopped what they were doing and just watched her. As they turned into his office, she glanced around to all the eyes. "Charlie, why is everyone just watching me? Do they know about Eli's affair with Tabby too?"

"Wait, what?" Charlie had no clue about the affair. "What affair? They are all probably wondering if their job is safe or not."

"Yeah, so Eli had an affair with his assistant, Tabby. It began on top of his desk. Why would their jobs not be safe?"

"He did what?" Charlie was fuming.

"He bought a house and car for Tabby, had an affair, said he was fixing our marriage, but instead he was having his cake and eating it too. Oh, and has another baby coming with her," MaryAnn just blurted it out. "So now, why are they worried about their jobs? What would I have anything to do with that?"

"MaryAnn, first off, I am sorry to hear my nephew did such a thing. He was not raised that way."

"Wait, what? Nephew?"

"Eli never told you, I am his father's brother."

"I barely knew his parents. He didn't talk about his family, let alone introduce me to anyone other than his mother's sister." She took a deep breath. "I didn't even know him like I thought I did."

"Well, I have been trying to get you to come in because with Eli's father gone and because he had a family, Eli became the majority owner to the dealership. Had his father knew Eli would screw off, he would have lost that share."

"Come to think about it, his affair started a month or two after his father's death." A light bulb went off; MaryAnn put it all together.

"When did Eli buy the house with Tabby?" Charlie sat down at his desk, pulling a file out.

"A month before his death, that is what she said."

Charlie looked up at MaryAnn then Jacob.

"Yes, we found her. Yes, MaryAnn confronted Tabby in the very home that was bought." Jacob interrupted before Charlie could ask. "For the record, I was Eli's best friend, and not once did he say to me that you were his uncle. Why keep it a secret?"

"Jacob, I have no clue. But I do know the timeline adds up. Around that time, Eli took a large withdraw from his share of the company, something the accountant would have caught when we did our annual audit. When I heard about the fire, I pulled up the account info. I was going to send you a check, you know, since I could not get you in here."

"Why would I get that money? It was his."

"Yes, his but now yours as the widow. See, MaryAnn, with the passing of Eli, you as his wife inherited this dealership, his portion. That is why everyone out there is sitting on their edge of their seat. We did not know what you planned to do with this dealership. If you kept it or if you were going to sell it out. Change is something our people are not looking forward to."

"I own this place, alongside with you?"

"Yes, and when I go, my son, he will take my share."

"Eli's cousin?"

"Yes."

"Where is he now?"

"Matthew is my go-to guy here. He runs the floor when needed, takes care of the shop when the shop manager is out. He makes sales when we are busy and need an extra hand. I have been teaching him this dealership since he was in his mom's belly."

"How old is he?"

Jacob looked at her. He can see in her eyes that she was contemplating something.

"Matthew is thirty-two. He is a father to two amazing kids, both six, they are twins. He also is a youth pastor for our church, just over the ridge."

"What are these papers you need me to sign about?"

"Some are renewal contracts for our salesmen, one is to upgrade some things in the shop. Another is for annual raises of some of the non-sales employees."

"What if I told you, I do not want the dealership? It is where I met Eli. I really do not want anything from the man I didn't even know."

"I would say, I wish I could buy you out, but I can't. Eli was the one making big here. I am only getting 5 percent. Eli held 95 percent, only because it was in his father's will that I was to keep some of it, something Eli was not happy about at all."

"Which is totally wrong. It should have gone fifty-fifty."

"That's what it once was." Charlie looked down at his desk. "I understand if you want to sell it to someone. I just ask that you make sure everyone is able to keep their job."

"What if I didn't want to sell it?"

Jacob just looked at Mary. He knew exactly where she was going.

"Mary, are you sure?"

She reached out and placed her hand on his.

"Jacob, it is the right thing to do."

"Am I missing something?" Charlie looked at them.

"No. Charlie, I do not want to sell the dealership. It is not mine to sell. You and your brother built this to what it is from the ground up. Eli never told me about how he got it, he never told me Matthew was his cousin and that you are his uncle. So many secrets of his are being exposed as the minutes pass by. I am a widow to a complete stranger. Charlie, what if I told you, I rather just turn the dealership over to you, 100 percent? Only thing I ask for is helping to get a decent running car. The only thing I came for."

Charlie dropped his pen. He did not understand what was going on. He just sat there, frozen.

"Jacob, please go find Matthew and have him come in here."

"Okay." Jacob left the room, closing the door behind him.

"MaryAnn."

"No, call me Mary. Family calls me Mary."

"Okay, Mary. Are you sure you want to do this?"

"I own a beauty shop. What do I need a dealership for? This is yours. This is your dealership. Your son should inherit it all. So what do we do? How do we do all of this?"

"I will need you to come back with the lawyer here. He will do all the paperwork and you will just need to sign it."

"That works for me."

Jacob returned with Matthew.

"Hey, Dad, everything okay?"

"Everything is great. Prayers have been answered, son. I tell ya, our God is mysterious and works in ways we can never figure out. He sent us an angel today. Mary, SUV or car?"

"What?"

"Tell me, if you had a choice, SUV or car?"

"Car since that is what I can afford."

"But she loves the expeditions," Jacob spoke up.

"Can't afford that, Jacob, and no, you're not helping me with that either."

"Color?"

"Silver gray is pretty nice, no leather, but seriously, I will look and find something I can afford."

"Matthew, lot twenty-nine. Keys and folder, complete folder."

"Dad?"

"I will explain in a second. Mary, are you truly sure about this?"

"Truly." She smiled. "Let's gather everyone in the main lobby. I want to break the news. I want to relax everyone who is worried. I feel really good about this."

"Okay." Charlie picked up the phone, trying to hold back his excitement. He made an announcement over the intercom. "I need everyone, sales members, team members, shop members, cleaners, all members of the dealership to the main lobby for an emergency meeting."

"Well, that is going to make them worried to all heck." Mary giggled.

"Dad, what is going on?"

"It's a good thing, Matthew, do not panic." MaryAnn looked at him. "By the way, I am Mary."

"Nice to finally meet you, Mary." Matthew took a breath and walked out the door. You can tell he was just a tad worried. Jacob followed Matthew, along with MaryAnn and Charlie.

Walking into main lobby, everyone stood there, with fear. Nobody said a word. They just watched her movement.

"Hey, everyone, thank you for showing up as fast as you did. I have a big announcement to make."

Mary stood on a chair. "We have a big announcement." She took a deep breath and started to speak. "I am MaryAnn, wife, well, widow of Eli. I came today just to get a new car and found out I inherited all of you and this. Yet I do not want this. I do not want anything to have to do with Eli. A person I came to find out I didn't even truly know after all these years, like how Charlie was his uncle and Matthew was his cousin. How he totally took Charlie's percentage of this dealership away. Well, you can all just breathe, for I am not selling this dealership. We are having papers drawn up, I am giving Charlie back his share, and I am signing papers over that Charlie gets all of the shares. Charlie, this dealership is yours. It always has been." Looking over, she noticed Matthew walking back into the room with a folder in his hands. "Matthew, you and your dad build this place up even more. Take it to a new level, keep God first. Make sure you treat each and every employee as though they were your family. God answered your prayers and helped me to find me again."

Everyone stood there, in pure shock.

"Are you sure, MaryAnn?" Matthew took a deep breath. "I mean, are you sure?"

"Yes, yes, I am, Matthew. I have never been so sure in my life. For once, something feels good, something that once was connected to Eli." Taking a deep breath, she looked over to Jacob. "We know all things work together for good for those who love God. To those who are called according to his purpose [Romans 8:28]. I truly believe that all of the tragic events that have happened in my life has led me here, to right the wrong that was done, to make sure everything is restoring to its former glory."

"Does that mean we will get our vacation time back?" one of the staff members spoke out.

"What?"

"Eli, when he took over, he canceled all of our benefits: our sick time, our vacation time, our insurance. Made us commission so that by law he did not have to provide all of that. He made promises that we would make a lot of money, but somehow even with the sales, we made less. Most of the staff only stayed because Charlie asked us to wait, that things will get better."

MaryAnn looked at Charlie with a horrific eye. He lowered his head, knowing this was all true.

"Charlie, is this…"

"I am sorry to say, MaryAnn, but it is. He cut back on so much to make himself more money."

"To spend on his mistress," MaryAnn said in sheer anger. Turning her attention back to the employees, she said, "I am truly sorry about all of this. I did not know. I did not know about any of this."

"I will make sure to remove the commission, return the hourly wage, and return the benefits to all the employees, MaryAnn. It is my turn to right the wrong."

A round of applause erupted the whole room.

"Good. You make sure you do that. Good luck to you all. Sell some cars. Keep God and your family first. Remember, you are all a family here."

"And you, MaryAnn, you remember you are part of our family. You are more to us than Eli ever was. His father would be so disappointed in him, and I am sure he is letting him know that." The employee stepped forward.

"What is your name?"

"Steve, Miss."

"Well, Steve, it is nice to meet you. What do you do here?"

"I help out with the shop when they need coverage, and I have been part of the sales team since Eli's father started the dealership. So to say his father would be disappointed in the person he became, I can say for fact. I watched Eli grow, his father was so proud of his son, and then later in life he started a slippery slope until you walked into the picture."

"I understand. He was a nice man, unlike his son. That is why Charlie will fix this."

"Yes, Matthew and I will take care of it all. Steve is right, MaryAnn. You, Dee, and Jacob, you three will forever be family and family takes care of one another. Just remember that. With that being said, everyone needs to get back to work. We have some transitioning to do. Steve, call all the old sales team members and shop members. Tell them it is time to come home. Matthew, pull the truck around."

"It's right out front, Dad."

"What truck?" Mary looked over at Charlie. "Charlie, I can't afford a new SUV."

"Just walk with me. I want to show you something. Jacob, you too." Charlie smirked as he led MaryAnn and Jacob out through the main doors to the dealership. Matthew trailed behind them.

There, parked on the sidewalk, a brand-new Ford Expedition, gray silver with the complete trim package.

"Charlie, I cannot afford this."

"I know, that is why it is yours. A thank you. Thank you for being honest, for being the person to fix years of damage all in one day. Before you say anything, sit inside. Check it out."

"Charlie, I can't."

"MaryAnn, you can, and you will. You are the most deserving person I know in this world. Now go check out the interior. If you do not like this one, then we can go find the one you really do."

"That won't be necessary." MaryAnn walked over to the Expedition. Opening the front door, she slid onto the driver's seat. She could not believe it: fully loaded with clothed seats. Touch screen, automatic third-row seating, separate rear entertainment system in headrests. "Charlie, this is beautiful."

"You look good in it," Jacob spoke up. "Real good in it. This is you, Mary."

"MaryAnn, enjoy it. Thank you for giving us hope back."

"Matthew, you are welcome."

"Here are the keys, the title, everything you need to know. Just come back inside and sign the temporary plates, call your insurance, get it put on, and drive off. Bring it back to get it serviced. We will take care of it."

"I will at least pay for service."

"Discounted if you insist on paying." Charlie grinned. "Jacob, take good care of Mary."

"I will." He reached his hand out and shook Matthew's hand.

"Good. We both know she deserves it."

MaryAnn walked into the dealership behind Matthew to sign some papers and get a hold of her insurance company.

The rest of the afternoon flew. MaryAnn could not believe she is driving off the dealership lot in a brand-new Expedition. Things are finally looking up, for now. It was not too long before she pulled up into Jacob's driveway. Without missing a beat, Jacob quickly parked his truck, jumped out just in time to open her driver's door.

"Jacob, you know you do not have to get my door every single time."

"Mary, yes I do." Jacob took her hand. "Come with me. I want to talk to you before Dee gets home."

"Okay." Mary followed his lead to the back corner of the yard, where he had a bench. "What's wrong, Jacob?"

"Mary, after today, after all the events, it has made it even more clear to me just how much I need to be here for you, not because I need to, not because I have to be, but because I want to be here for you. Give you the life you deserved to have but was cheated out of. Give you the love that you deserve. I know we said we were going to take things slowly, but I just want you to realize that I love you. I have always loved you and I will always love you even if you never do."

"Jacob, I—"

"I know, you need time. I understand."

"No, Jacob, that is not what I was about to say."

Just at that moment they were interrupted by Mary's phone ringing.

"Ugh." Mary sighed. "Hello?"

"Hello, MaryAnn?"

"Yes, this is MaryAnn."

"Hi, this is Assistant Principal Morris. I have Deanna here in the office. I need to speak with you on a matter that happened today as school was to be let out. I cannot let her go with Mrs. Stacy Shell."

"Is she okay?"

"She is."

"Okay, I am on my way." MaryAnn stood up. "Jacob, can we finish this conversation later. I must get to the school. Something happened and the assistant principal needs to see me."

"Do you want me to come with you?"

"No, I need to handle this, whatever this is."

"Okay. Call me, please, when you're done."

"I will." Mary kissed Jacob's cheek. "I promise, when I get back, we will finish this talk."

Jacob put his hand on his cheek where Mary kissed him. He watched as she turned and ran to her new truck. Putting it in reverse, he watched as she sped off down the road. He grabbed his phone and called Stacy.

"Hey, Jacob."

"What is going on?"

"I don't know. Mark was called to the school, and he called me to tell me not to pick up Dee. I was just getting ready to call you."

"Is the school on lockdown?"

"No, buses are loading as normal."

"I don't know what is going on. Mary just flew out of here."

"I hope Dee is okay."

"Me too."

Mary threw her four-ways on, letting everyone know she had urgent matter she was rushing to. The school really was not too far from the house; she was there in matter of moments. Pulling into a parking spot, she spotted the ambulance driver and Mark standing at the front doors. Buses were pulling out, taking students home.

"Mark!" MaryAnn yelled as she ran up to the door.

"Mary."

"Is Dee okay? What the heck is going on?"

"Dee is fine. Why don't we head to the principal's office? Jerry, you're cleared if you want to head back to the squad."

"You got it, Chief. See ya, MaryAnn."

"Bye, Jerry." MaryAnn waved as she nervously walked behind Mark. They walked into the front door and around the corner to the assistant principal's office. There, MaryAnn spotted Deanna sitting just outside of the office with an ice pack on her face.

"Deanna!" MaryAnn ran to her daughter. "What happened?"

"Ms. Baker, can we talk in my office please?" Assistant Principal Morris stepped out. MaryAnn just looked at Deanna as she followed both Mark and Mr. Morris into the office. "Ms. Baker…"

"MaryAnn please."

"MaryAnn, this is Mrs. Jones, Samantha's mother."

"Natalie." Mrs. Jones stood up to shake MaryAnn's hand.

"Reason I called for you two in here today, well, both girls are suspended for the rest of the week, for fighting."

"FIGHTING?" MaryAnn exclaimed. "Deanna has never hurt anything, not even a fly."

"We are all pretty shocked too, MaryAnn. Deanna is one of our most quiet, loving, helpful students."

"So what happened?"

"Natalie, from the three teachers and our resource officer, apparently your daughter has been taunting Deanna throughout the day. Making remarks that they set the fire to the house for more attention. From my reports, Samantha pushed Deanna to the ground, telling her that her mother was a fake, and that she deserved to be cheated on, throwing dirt at Deanna while she was on the ground, yelling at her saying she would never be anything to her dead father. The one teacher stated as she started to walk over to stop all this, Deanna got to her feet and threw her fists. We called for an ambulance to check on both girls. Chief Shell has to come out when something this major goes down."

"MaryAnn, I am so sorry my daughter said all those things." Natalie put her head down.

"It took two teachers and our officer to pull Deanna off Samantha." Mr. Morris looked at MaryAnn. "Is there more to her anger than hearing words?"

"Mr. Morris, she lost her father, she lost her home. She found out her father was not faithful. He had a whole another family other than ours. She has a lot of anger built up. We pray over it, but I just think the harsh words just tipped her over the edge. Natalie, why would Samantha taunt her?"

"I am ashamed to admit, but your husband's mistress is my sister. I stopped talking to her when I learned she was messing with a married man. I told her to stop, that was not how we were raised. I guess with our disagreement, Samantha was taking it out on your daughter. I am not making excuses, nor am I condoning such hatred, but that is the only reason I can think of as to why Sam would do such a thing."

"Well, let us bring them both in here. Let us have a chat," Mark spoke up. Mark opened the door and motioned for them to come into the office. He motioned for Deanna to sit in the one chair next to MaryAnn and for Samantha to sit next to her mother.

"Sammy, why? Just why?" Natalie did not want to wait. "Why such hatred words, acts?"

"Mom, seriously? You have no room to talk. You disowned your own sister for falling in love."

"How does that have anything to do with me?" Deanna scolded.

"Deanna, quiet. You're in enough trouble."

"Yeah, Deanna, listen to your mommy."

"Samantha Marie Jones, I have had enough of your outbursts. What you said and have done all day is uncalled for and will not be tolerated. Not only are you suspended. You are also grounded for the rest of the month. Give me your phone, no school dance or after-school activities. You are to go to school and come right home. I will be bringing you and picking you up. Take her off the team. I am pulling her, Mr. Morris. You wait! We will be stopping at your father's job. He will hear about all of this."

"Mom!"

"No! You do not knock a person down when they are already down. I am so extremely disappointed in you! MaryAnn, Deanna, I am terribly sorry for my daughter's selfish acts. If she even glances your way, or any of her 'mighty' friends glance your way, I will handle it."

"Mom, you can't pull me from the team!"

"Actually, Samantha, she can. I will let the coach know tomorrow morning."

"I forgive you." Deanna looked over at Samantha. "The Lord teaches us to forgive, so I forgive you. I will pray for you as well."

"You are right, Dee. He does teach us to forgive. Mark, Mr. Morris, I am sorry for my daughter's outburst. It will not happen again. She will see you Monday morning with a better outlook on life. Natalie, good luck. We will pray for you and your sister. I think you should make amends with your sister too. She needs you now more than ever."

Natalie looked over at MaryAnn with a confused look.

"Just trust me. Go see her. I forgive her too."

Natalie got up. Taking Samantha, they left the office. As MaryAnn and Deanna stood, Mark motioned them to stop.

"What you two just did, forgiving someone, is why this community loves you both so much. Mary, Deanna was defending herself. Be easy on her. From the investigation, that is a fact."

"I know. Take her home with you. Stacy was really disappointed that their girls' shopping trip was cut out. It does not have to be. Deanna, this does not mean you are out of the woods though."

"I know."

"How is your face?"

"It's fine. A little bruised but I am okay." Deanna gave her mother a hug. "Are we going to be okay, Mom?"

"Yes, we are. We will be fine." MaryAnn hugged her daughter back, shook Mr. Morris's hand, and headed out the door. She watched Deanna walk to the cruiser with Mark. Deanna gave her a little wave and off they went.

Taking a deep breath, she got into her new SUV. She sat for a moment, and that is when the flood gates opened. She never thought in a million years her tragic moments would catch up and affect her daughter at school.

"Okay, Lord, I lift it all to you." She closed her eyes and she prayed. "I lift every bit up to you. I admit, although I lean on my faith, I have not been true to you or myself since that moment I left my home with my grandparents for the last time. You can only pretend so much and now, Lord. I cannot pretend anymore. Please do not let this trickle down to my daughter, Lord. I have to let go and lift it all to you: my anger, my hurt, my distrust, I lift it all to you." She took a deep breath, wiping her the tears from her eyes. Then she did something she has not since that very day: she sang out loud: "Amazing Grace."

CHAPTER 9

Back to the Drawing Boards

MaryAnn drove out of the school parking lot. Still lost in her own thoughts, she just drove. From losing her husband to learning that he was not the man who she thought he was, finding out who her mystery man from high school is, losing her home and car in a fire, only to find out that her child home was still hers and locked in time all in a short time. Just shaking her head, MaryAnn pulled from her thoughts to realize she was sitting in her driveway, her childhood home.

"What do I do with this place?" Just staring at the front door, she hesitated to get out of the truck. "I just don't know what to do." Taking a deep breath, turning off the engine, taking her seatbelt off, she slid out of the seat.

"Excuse me, MaryAnn?" a soft female's voice came from behind.

MaryAnn jumped a little.

"Oh, I am sorry, I did not mean to startle you."

"That's okay. I did not know you were behind me."

"My name is Doris. Your mother and I, we were awfully close. I am not sure if you remember me."

"Aunt Doris?"

"Yep, that is me. Well, that is what you used to call me." She smiled.

"I haven't seen you since—"

"Since we said farewell to your parents. I tried to reach out, but I left messages and did not hear back. After a while I stopped trying to reach out, but just know I did not stop thinking about you, kiddo. We prayed for you."

"Uncle Tom."

"Yep. He is a few houses down, visiting with our daughter and her baby. When I saw you pull up into the driveway, I knew I had to come say hi. I wanted to know if you were okay. Our daughter, Beth, she has told me everything that has been going on over the past few months. Well, everything that is hearsay passes down."

"Well, honestly, I am slightly confused." MaryAnn headed for the porch; Doris followed. They both sat down on the swing. "I am just learning that I own this house. I just saw it earlier today for the first time since the day we said farewell. It's just as it was inside, the day they died. From the plates in the strainer to their bed."

"What are you slightly confused about?"

"Long story short, first day of high school, a boy, Jacob, stole my heart, but I didn't know it was Jacob. Later on in life, I would meet his best friend, not knowing he was the kid from that only day of public school I had. I would fall in love and marry him, but he would die tragically the same way my parents did at the same very spot, only to learn he had an affair and was starting another family with another woman. I would learn that his best friend, my friend Jacob, was the kid from school, that he has known who I was since day one when Eli introduced us and is still madly in love with me. I would lose my house in a fire and at this point staying with him, not sure what to do. Oh yeah, and my daughter who would never hurt a fly got into a brutal fight with the niece of the mistress at school today." Just staring blankly off into the sky, MaryAnn spoke, "I am sorry, Aunt Doris. I didn't mean to blurt all that out. I haven't seen you in forever."

"Oh, my sweet child, you have been given a heck of a hand to deal with and no one really to open up to. I just wish I came to you sooner or found you sooner. I am so sorry you had to go through all this. Can I ask you something?"

"Yes."

"What do you want? What do you want out of life?"

"I don't know." MaryAnn looked over at Doris.

"Search, deep inside, my dear, you know." Doris, wise in her years, wanted to help in any way she could, pushing MaryAnn to open up and realize what she genuinely wants. "Close your eyes and ask yourself, what is your heart saying. It is time you put yourself first, not what you think should be right or what feels need to be done to be right. Put yourself first."

"Aunt Doris, I have a daughter I need to put first though."

"Not while you are slightly confused, or lost, you need to put yourself first. Trust this almost eighty-year-old. I have been around for some time now. Now, close your eyes."

MaryAnn closed her eyes.

"Now take a deep breath and slowly let it out."

She took a deep breath and let it out.

"Now, where do you see yourself?"

"Here, but the house is redone."

"What else do you see?"

"My daughter, smiling, being free."

"How do you feel?"

"Happy, relaxed, at peace."

"Anything else that you can see or feel?"

"Jacob. He is there with us. I feel safe." MaryAnn opened her eyes. "How did you do that?"

"What? Get you to open your mind, your heart?"

"Yeah. I have been praying and praying, talking to God, to myself, trying to figure this all out and you find me. Within five to ten minutes you have me feeling very content."

"Well, I was once a therapist, counselor. So you can say, I know what I am doing." Doris chuckled. "I have been retired for about thirty years."

MaryAnn let out a laughter.

"Well, okay then. Aunt Doris, what would you think my parents would say about all this?"

"I am sure they would want you to be happy. That is all they wanted for you when they were physically here. That is why they let you go to public school. They knew it would make you happy. So, my dear child, be happy." She placed her hand onto MaryAnn's. "So what are you going to do?"

"First, I am going to give you a big hug! Thank you so much!" MaryAnn did just that. "Now, I am going to go into the house and begin the long process of clearing it out. I am going to try to donate as much as I can and then repaint, remodel with what little funds I have, and move in. The quicker I can get in, the better Deanna and I will be."

"Deanna?"

"My daughter. How long are you and Uncle Tom in town for?"

"For two weeks. We just got here yesterday."

"Okay, good. I want you to meet Deanna."

"And I want to meet this Jacob."

MaryAnn's phone began to ring.

"Speaking of Jacob." She answered the phone. "Hey."

"Hey. Are you okay?"

"I am now."

"What does that mean? Stacy called asking if they could take Deanna out to eat, not sure if she was grounded or not. I told them to go ahead, that you were not home yet."

"Oh, Jacob, I am sorry. I did not mean to worry you. I am at my parents' house, catching up with one of my mom's dearest friends, Aunt Doris."

"As long as you are okay, that is all that matters to me. Hey, Mary, why would Dee be grounded?"

"Well, let's just say she can help us at the house for the next few days. She got suspended for fighting in school."

"WHAT?" Jacob darn near dropped his phone. "Is she okay? What happened?"

"Well, obviously she is okay. She is shopping with Stacy," Mary sarcastically said, trying to lighten the mode. "Why don't you come over? I want to go over a few things with you and Aunt Doris wants to meet you."

"Okay. Let me get my shoes on."

"I'll order a pizza."

"Mary, you're okay though."

"Jacob, I am better than ever. Come over here please."

"On my way." Jacob hung up the phone. Grabbing his keys, tossing his shoes on, he was out the door before Mary could hit end on her phone.

"Well, if you sit tight for a minute, Jacob will be here. By the sounds of it, he was already out the door before I hung up."

"That man really cares for you."

"He sure does. He should have been the one I started my life out with."

"Make sure he is the one you finish your life with then. I hope you still do read the Bible."

"I lean on the Good Book, Aunt Doris. It is what has helped me through these tough times."

"That would make your mama and daddy extremely happy and proud. The one thing that was the strongest in their life was their faith. It always came first above all."

"Aunt Doris, is there anything inside you would like? From Mommy and Daddy?"

"No, my child, everything I need or want is here." She patted her heart and her head. "In my heart forever and my memories till the end. Anything else would just be an item, something left behind for someone else to deal with. At my age, no need for that."

"That makes a lot of sense."

"Sometimes something means more to one person than it does the other. It's their memories, not yours. So keep that in mind as you go through your parents' items. That might help you with donating more than you think."

"Thank you, Aunt Doris. That helps a lot." MaryAnn looked up to see Jacob pulling into the driveway, next to her truck. "That makes a lot of sense." She could not help herself but to start to shine, to smile.

"This must be your beat to your heart, the reason to your smile, or another catchphrase, the shine to that glow in your face," Aunt Doris whispered.

"It is." MaryAnn watched Jacob as he got out of the vehicle and walked up the porch steps. "Hey."

"Hey." Not even noticing the elderly lady sitting next to her, Jacob kept his eyes locked onto Mary's. Something was different this time, the way she was looking at him.

"Jacob, this is Aunt Doris. She was a very dear friend of my mother."

"Hello, Aunt Doris. It is very nice to meet you." Breaking his eye contact with Mary, he walked over and reached his hand out to shake hers.

"Likewise." She smiled at him. "MaryAnn, I am going to head back up to Beth's house. Will you be around tomorrow?"

"Yes, I have a lot of work to do."

"Good, Uncle Tom and I will be down."

"Good, I would love to see him. Thank you so much for coming up. I don't know why my grandparents never told me you called, but I am glad to have you here now."

"Yes, I do not know why either, but I am glad I was able to see you again. Jacob, will you be here as well tomorrow?"

"Well, it sounds like Mary has a lot of work to do, so yes, I will be here to help her out."

"Good, Uncle Tom will want to meet you as well. Until then, have a lovely night."

Jacob reached his hand out to help Doris up. She gave them both a hug and left Jacob and Mary alone on the steps. The feeling in the air was different. Jacob could not figure it out.

"Jacob, we need to talk." Mary looked at him as she turned, headed back to the swing.

Jacob's stomach flopped. Usually when a girl makes that comment, "We need to talk," it's either the girl is pregnant, which in this case is not possible with him, or they want to end whatever they have going on.

"Okay." Nervously he sat next to her on the porch swing.

"Jacob, I am completely head over heels in love with you." She noticed the color returning to his pale face. "It was you who I was supposed to start my life with, but the winds changed, and now it's you to whom I want to finish the rest of my life with. Knowing that, I do not want to jump. I want us to walk, to enjoy this new adventure, our adventure. I want to live in my parents' house, but I want it to be ours. I want your help and input with remodeling it..."

"But?"

"But I don't want us to just jump into living together."

"But you see us living together later on."

"I see us being the family we should have always been."

"Mary, that is all I need to hear. We can go as slow or as fast as you want it, as long as I know we have a future together."

"Jacob, we do, we so do." She placed her hands into his. "It's us."

"Yes, it's us." He gently squeezed her hands. "Well, what shall we do?"

"Start to clean the house out." Mary giggled. "First, I need to call Stacy and let her know to bring Deanna here."

"While you do that, would you like me to call for pizza?"

"That works since I never called for the pizza." MaryAnn stood up; Jacob followed. "Hey, Jacob, thank you for waiting, for understanding."

"Anything for you." He slid his hands to her cheeks, gently bringing his lips to meet hers. A soft gentle kiss. "MaryAnn, I loved you then and I will forever love you to the end. What would you like on your pizza?"

"You are just truly romantic." Smiling from ear to ear, MaryAnn returned the kiss with a little chuckle. "What about sausage?"

"Oh, just wait, I am going to treat you and show you what love is truly about."

Jacob's hands moved from MaryAnn's cheeks, sliding them to her waist as he lifted her in the air, swing her in a circle. She let out a playful screech before letting her back down again. Catching her balance, she looked into his eyes. This felt right, so very right. Reaching for her phone, she headed for the front door.

"Hey, Stacy, it's Mary."

"Hey, Mary. We are just getting dinner, did some good shopping too."

"Sounds like fun."

"And of course, my husband went into police mode and had a stern talk to her about the fight in school. I am truly sorry about that."

"Oh my, it's perfectly okay. She needed that for sure. When you guys bring her home, bring her to my house, my childhood home. That is where Jacob and I will be."

"Oh."

"It's time, time to go back to the drawing boards, restart, hit the reset button on life."

"I understand, Mary. The best way to do that is to go where it all began."

"Exactly."

"Well, we will take our time and bring her over as soon as we are done."

"See you then." MaryAnn hung up the phone.

Turning the key, she walked into the living room. Waves of emotions just returned to her as she looked around. Taking a deep breath, she closed her eyes, visualizing on what the final outcome will be. An open floor plans. Light tan walls. Her photos on the walls. The fireplace mantel with her parents' picture on it. New kitchen. Rooms repainted.

"Mary, you okay?"

"Oh, hey. Yeah, I am okay, Jacob. Just thinking of the changes I would like to do."

"Tell me your ideas."

"Can this wall come down? Make it more open?"

"Well, I will have to look to see if it can, but if it can't, we can always make a decorative post out of it. You know, close this part of that goes into the hallway, arch out a support beam, and open the wall that way. You can get to the hallway from the kitchen area."

"I actually like the sounds of that. The bedroom area should be more private to the family anyway. There is a half bathroom off the kitchen as well, so no need to access the bedroom hallway."

"Okay, so we have that idea. What else, Mary? What else can you see?" Jacob walked up behind Mary, placing a hand on each side of her waist.

"The rooms, instead of this dark dingy color, more like a light tan, brighten the room up. These photos and decorations would come down. What photos of Dee and I that I can print off will be on the walls. A few photos of just my parents on the fireplace mantel. The kitchen, redone. With the wall opened up, I can put an island in the kitchen and new cabinets and sank in sink."

"I am loving it."

"But for now, I guess just a new paint job is all that I will be able to do."

"Why do you say that, Mary?"

"Money, time."

"Now you know you will not need to worry about that."

"And I am not asking for any help or donations either, Jacob. You know that is not me."

"I know, my love, I know." Jacob looked into her eyes. "You are so humble, one of the many amazing features I truly love about you, but if help shows up, it would be rude to turn them away."

"Jacob."

"I am not contacting anyone." Jacob smirked.

"Promise me, Jacob."

"Okay, I promise." Jacob leaned in and gave Mary a quick peck. "So let's start packing up the house. We can use one room as a keep and one room as a donate until we get bags or boxes."

"Okay. That sound likes a plan. Let us start with this wall, here, so that you can start to take the wall down. The furniture is going. Donate that so we can move that to the opposite side of the room."

"Why don't we put the furniture in the garage, along with all other big items that you will be donating?"

"Good idea, Jacob." MaryAnn smiled. "Let me go open up the garage door and we can do that right now. I am not sure what is in there though."

"Not much, just a work bench."

"Perfect. Let us move both the couch and love seat in there along with the tables as well. We can leave the kitchen table for now, for a spot to eat at."

"Sounds like a plan."

It did not take long to move the couches and tables out. MaryAnn took all the photos and decorations from the tables, walls, and mantle and laid them on her parents' bed. Her parents' room would be the last to do. The room looked bigger.

"So are we going to knock the wall down or build the arch?"

"Jacob, I love your idea. Let us go ahead and start to tear the wall down, leaving the studs up. We have three huge trash cans in the back we can put the debris in."

"Why don't you get them, and I will start to remove the trim and outlet covers?" Jacob grabbed the tool bag that was sitting by the door.

Music going, hammer hitting the wall, debris being tossed in the garbage can. Engrossed in the current project, they did not hear the door being knocked on.

"Excuse me, Mr. Shaffer, your order!" the pizza driver shouted above the music and demolition.

"Oh, Tony! Sorry, we didn't hear you knock."

"That's okay, sir, here is your pie."

Jacob took the pizzas and gave Tony a tip.

"Doing some remodeling?"

"Yep," MaryAnn spoke up, purely excited. "Making this home my own, well it is, but updating it."

"That is awesome. Well, if you would like some help, I can paint. I love this kind of thing. We just redid my parents' house. Just let me know!"

"Oh, Tony, you are so sweet, but—"

"We would never refuse help. It would be rude, so we would love the help whenever you can. All the rooms are being stripped and repainted. I know you know what you are doing, you know, with your dad owning his own construction company and all," Jacob spoke up, giving Tony a hint of a wink.

"Perfect. I will give you a call tomorrow! Dad still have your number, Mr. Shaffer?"

"He sure does." Jacob shook Tony's hand. "Thanks, Tony. Tell your dad hello for me."

"Will do."

Tony left the house, just as Mark and Stacy walked in.

"Jacob, I—"

"I know you are not asking for help or donations, but he offered."

"Ugh. Okay."

"Was that Joe's kid Tony?" Mark asked he walked in the door.

"Yeah, just dropped off pizza."

"Wow, you guys cleared this room out quickly." Mark took notice to the wall halfway down.

"Yeah, I decided, before Dee and I move in, we need to remodel. I was only going to do a paint job, you know with money and time, but Jacob insists on making my visions come true."

"Mom, what house is this?"

"Hey, Dee, so this is my childhood home. This is the house I grew up in. We are going to live here after we repaint and do some home makeover things. Jacob and I, we are in the process in taking this wall down, extending the hallway a little. Then I would like to repaint, update the light fixtures, and remodel the bathrooms as well as the kitchen. Kitchen first once we finish this living room."

"This is the house your parents owned?"

"Yes. We are going to donate all the furniture too. I want to start fresh. Begin our new life, in my childhood home, with new memories."

"I love that idea, Mom! When can we go pick out colors? Furniture too?"

"Well, it depends how fast the land sells where our burned-out house is. The faster that sells, the quicker we can shop and remodel. I had Jacob put it on the market for me today. I just have to stop tomorrow to sign the paperwork."

"Can we create a wish list? I mean, go to the hardware store and pick out the colors and the furniture store next door... Just look, Mom? It is not too late."

"Dee, it's seven. I do not think the stores are open."

"Well, the hardware store is in the same shopping center as the furniture store. They both close at ten, plenty enough time."

"Yeah, I can go with you, girls' trip. Jacob knows what you want done. So what do you say?"

"I look like a hot mess."

"You look beautiful. Go clean up and enjoy some time with the girls." Jacob brushed the hair from MaryAnn's face.

"Ugh, okay. I guess we can go. Stacy, you don't mind driving, do you?"

"Nope, I do not mind driving. Let's go."

"Let me grab a slice of pizza to go."

Twenty minutes later, MaryAnn, Dee, and Stacy headed into town, leaving Mark and Jacob behind.

"So, Mark, let me show you all that she wants to do and flat out told me most would have to wait due to time and money."

"She knows she can ask, and everyone would gladly pitch in."

"I was told not to ask. She didn't want handouts. She has great pride and independence. So I told her if someone offers to help, then it would be rude to decline."

"Say no more. I got this. She can't deny all the help that is coming toward her. Let me call the hardware store. Anything she puts on the wish list is to be put aside as I will purchase it."

"Mark, you have to call the furniture store too. I can't tell a lie to her. I want to buy her furniture, but if you call and order it and just simply use my card, then it's not a lie when she asks if I bought it because you ordered. I can say no, I didn't."

"Very clever. Let me make a call to Joey too. He and Tony can really help. We can have this remodel done in a day or two."

"Tony already offered to help, so I am sure they would do it in a heartbeat."

"Good, let's go over everything. I want to write it down."

The girls made it quickly to town, going over color swatch after color swatch.

"What do you think, Dee? This color for the kitchen? It's like a nice pale yellow."

"I like it. What about this color for my room? It's more like a light sky blue."

"That's a pretty color. What about darker blue for an accent wall?" Stacy pointed out.

"I love that idea." MaryAnn smiled.

"MaryAnn, this is a pretty light tan for the living room and hallway."

"Yes, I like it, and maybe the next shade darker for the bathrooms."

"What about your room, Mom?"

"I was thinking a nice pale green, like a pastel."

"That would be pretty."

"Well, now we have colors picked, let us go look at a new kitchen. Mark texted me all the measurements."

"It's a pipe dream. We can do that another day."

"That is silly. Cory is back there waiting for us. I told him we were coming in. He is my nephew, so he will not be all salesman on us."

"Ugh, Stacy, I can't afford a new kitchen."

"That's fine. We can still create a wish list so you know what you have to work for."

"Ugh, you're right. At least I would know how much I need to save. I cannot believe you set this up this fast. Come on, Dee, let us go create a kitchen."

It did not take MaryAnn long to create a new kitchen, knowing exactly what she was looking for. Picked out the cabinets, all the extra drawers, the hardware for not just the kitchen but throughout the house. Next furniture.

"Hey, Tom."

"Hey, Stacy, what can I do for you today?"

"Well, eventually MaryAnn and Dee will be purchasing furniture for their whole house, but for now they are doing a wish list."

"Awesome. So, MaryAnn, should we start..."

"The living room Tom. I want something comfortable yet affordable. A couch, love seat, and maybe chair. Tables as well. Then the bedroom, single set for Deanna and myself, a queen set would be simply fine."

"I can work with that. Let me show you some options." Tom walked them around, from room to room.

MaryAnn sat on couch after couch until she found the perfect one. It did not take Deanna long to choose her bedroom set, coming with a desk and all. MaryAnn looked at a few before finding a beautiful set.

"These are all fine selections, and we will have them when you are ready. Also, for being a local business owner, we will take 25 percent off the final bill."

"Really?"

"Yes."

"Thank you, Tom. I just may be able to get this if the land sells fast."

"You are very welcome."

"Well, ladies, shall we head back to the house, see what the boys are up to?"

"Hopefully not too much."

Back at the house, Jacob and Mark were extremely busy.

"Okay, Jacob, they are on their way back. Stacy just texted me."

"So, Joe, what do you think? Is this something you can help me out?"

"For Mary, it would be my pleasure. Let me get out of here before she gets here. I will have a crew here tomorrow to get started. Just have her clear everything she can tonight."

"If it's in the garage and not on the work bench, it's to be donated."

"That works too. Good thinking, Jacob. I will contact the church and have them bring their truck over as well, get it out of there."

"Perfect. Thanks, Joe. Best you escape now. I don't want her to know we reached out."

"You got it, Mark." Joe shook the guys' hands and left, just in time.

Stacy pulled up just only a few minutes after Joe left.

"So what have you guys been up to?" MaryAnn walked into the living room, finding the wall completely down, cleaned up. "Well, you two work fast."

"What else were we going to do, stand here and dance?" Jacob chuckled. "So why don't we pack up some things you are going to donate? Get the photos off all the walls? It might help if we clean out the kitchen too so we can come in tomorrow and really detail clean it and you can reorganize the cabinets any way you want."

"Sounds like a good idea, Jacob, but it's almost nine."

"I have no school tomorrow, Mom, so no bedtime for me to worry about."

"Yeah, Dee, not for a good reason too."

"We can help," Stacy spoke up, feeling the tension begin to rise.

"No, I am not asking you to stay."

"Nonsense. We offered, and it would be rude to decline." Mark smiled as he grabbed a box.

"Where did all these boxes come from?" MaryAnn looked around.

In a quick response, Jacob spoke, not a lie, just not the whole truth, "Tony came back. They had these sitting around since the remodel on his parents' place. Figured you could use them." Which was the truth. Only part he left out was Joe being there, taking measurements, making calls to the lumber yard, the hardware store, and placing orders.

"Oh, that was genuinely nice of him. That kid will grow into a fine young man."

"Okay, let us get this party started. Mary, what you need to focus on is taking the boxes and, Mark, save on them. Dee, you will be running back and forth, take the things your mom is going to donate to the garage."

"Well, she can take some bags and just go into the bedrooms and empty all the clothes into them, donating every single bit of them. Start with my parents' room. That will be a huge help for me."

"That works. I can do that." Dee grabbed the box of bags and disappeared. She knew her mom would not handle this particular job so well.

"I will work in the kitchen." Stacy smiled as she grabbed a box and headed to the kitchen.

"Donate it all. Until I get new plates and whatnot, we can use paper plates and plastic silverware. Only thing I would like to keep would be my mom's baking items, the mixer, and bowls too."

"I am on it."

Everyone grabbed boxes and bags, music going, and they went to work. It did not take as long as MaryAnn expected to be. She walked back and forth, looking at things, picking to donate or to keep. Slowly the garage began to fill up. Deanna counted up to twenty-four bags of clothes between the two rooms and another three from the hall closet. Midnight came around and the last box left the house to the jam-packed garage. The house was empty. Ready to be repainted.

"It already looks different."

"Yes, it does, Dee. Let us head back to Jacob's place and get some sleep." MaryAnn hugged her daughter. It was a bittersweet feeling. Her family home was turning into her home; she only hoped and prayed her parents would approve.

"Don't you worry, Mary. They would be happy that you chose to live here and make it yours." Mark put his hand on her shoulder. "Your eyes tell me your thoughts."

She wiped a single tear away as they walked out of the house, not knowing this is the last time she will ever see it with the old kitchen, the old colored walls, the old flooring, not knowing that when she would return tomorrow, there would be a crew in the house demoing and replacing everything from the electrical to what plumbing needs updated to a whole new kitchen and roof. A whole new house with precious memories still living in there.

CHAPTER 10

A Year Later

It has been a year to the day when Jacob and Mark surprised MaryAnn with a complete home makeover. She is still in complete awe over it, pulling up to the house and seeing construction trucks left and right, people coming in and out of the house. Two whole dumpsters were filling up with debris. The church donation truck backed up to the garage, clearing it out. Everyone pausing when they saw MaryAnn standing there, then breaking out with applause and a huge surprise. Joe walking up, shaking her hand. "It will be rude to turn down help" were his exact words. Then and only then is when MaryAnn knew Jacob was involved. It was then her phone rang; the land had sold, with the burned-out house still there. Things were finally looking up for MaryAnn. Life was finally handing her cards she can handle.

"Good morning, Mary," Jacob said, stepping into the new open living room.

"Hey, Jacob, just in time for breakfast."

"Smells good. What did you make?"

"Eggs, English muffins, bacon, and sausage."

"All that for just you and Dee?"

"Nope, all that for us." Mary grabbed Jacob's hand, placing a kiss on his cheek, and led him to the table. "It has been one year since you have made this all happened."

"It wasn't just me."

"Mostly, I will forever be thankful."

*****

MaryAnn closed her eyes, thinking back, seeing all the kitchen items she picked out going into a storage container in her yard, seeing the furniture store unloading into the second storage container. She looked over at Jacob.

"Did you call everyone in town?"

"Nope, I did not make one single phone call." Which was the pure truth. The moment Mark and Stacy pulled out of the driveway, they were already on the phone, getting the storage pods delivered first thing, arranging things with Joe.

"Well, who did? It's only ten. When did they all get here?"

"We started promptly at six. The dumpsters showed up around seven and the pods around eight. Roofers were here by seven as well. We already got the kitchen completely gutted. The electrician is already rewiring the kitchen and then moving on to the rest of the house. Plumber is adjusting and replacing pipes. Stacy came up with the idea to take the back porch, turn it into a sunroom, and put on a new porch that would wrap around the sunroom and extend to the side of the house to the front, allowing multiple doors in the sunroom for you as well."

"Joe, you guys, how am I going to repay for all of this? What I am making off the land is not enough."

"We are asking that you host the first BBQ."

"No, I am being serious."

"So are all of us. We are all doing this out of love and respect for you. The kitchen was bought and paid for, the furniture was bought and paid for. Someone donated money for the roof. The wiring, the electrician is a father and son duo that your father helped their family out, and it's one way of repaying him back, and the list goes on and on. So no, we do not want your money. Remember Matthew 7:12: 'Therefore whatever you desire for men to do to you, you shall also do to them; for this is the law of the prophets.'"

"Well, thank you, Joe. How about I start today? Jacob can bring his grill over, and for lunch I will cook up some hot dogs and hamburgers. I can run to the store and get some salads and paper plates."

"Now, my lady, that sounds like a deal."

*****

"So a year later and you are still loving it?"

"I am, Jacob."

"Show me your favorite room." He smiled as she looked around.

"I love it all. I love my new living room, my island, and new kitchen setup. I am loving my new bathroom with the nice big tub. But if I had to choose my favorite room, it would be the sunroom." She took his hand and led him into the sunroom. The sun was peeking through the open windows, a slight breeze. She had a nice comfy corner chair with a small side table, her Bible lying next to her devotions. A small bookshelf against the one wall. She let go of Jacob's hand to walk over to the window, lowering it just a little. As she turned around, she lost her ability to breath, to focus. There, with his blue eyes looking directly into hers, on one knee, Jacob held out his one hand for hers with the other hand holding a box.

"MaryAnn Dunn, you are the most beautiful, amazing, inspiring person I have ever met. I knew from that moment you dropped your books in the hall that you are my one and only. I would love to spend each day showing you how loved you are, to wake up holding you in my arms every morning, to share each happy and sad moments and exciting moments too. I want to spend the rest of every second of my life with you, my true love. Will you please do me the honor in being my wife?"

MaryAnn stood in silence. She did not know what to say. It has only been a year. Was it too soon? Trying to find her words and the right answer, her thoughts were cut short.

"Mom, say yes already! I did!" Dee screeched from the doorway.

"You said yes? I am confused."

"He asked me on one knee if I would accept him as his stepfather and allow me to help you raise me. I said no. I would love if he would be my father."

"You asked for her blessing?" Tears began to stream down.

"I did." Jacob smiled. "So what do you say, Mary?"

"Yes. Yes. A hundred times over, I will marry you, Jacob!"

In one swift motion, Jacob picked up MaryAnn and swung her around as she squealed with pure excitement and joy. Deanna jumped for joy and ran to the door.

"SHE SAID YES!"

"Who is she yelling out the door to?" MaryAnn looked over as her feet hit the ground.

"Anyone who will listen!" Deanna smiled as she held the door open. Mark and Stacy walked in.

"Now you do not think we would have missed this moment for the world, right?" Mark walked in. Smiling, he hugged MaryAnn. "Congratulations. I am so happy for you!"

"We saw it all. Watched it like Peeping Toms through the window," Stacy openly admitted as she raced to hug Jacob. "I am so happy for the both of you. You both deserve to have that happily ever after, all three of you."

"Now she said yes, I think it is time to prep my house for the market."

"Are you sure?" MaryAnn looked at him.

"Yep, I am sure. Once we are married, I want our lives to begin as one, here, in your home."

"Our home." MaryAnn took his hand as she reached for Deanna's hand. "Our home."

The atmosphere to the room filled with warmth. Everyone just stood for a moment in silence. Reflection of the past to now filled MaryAnn's mind. The first day meeting Jacob in school, then marrying Eli, all the tragic events, the mistress and baby, to now. For the first time she truly was able to just breathe and let go, be happy. A pure moment of calm and peace.

"So we need to start to plan the wedding," Stacy broke the silence.

"No, I do not want it big. I want it sweet and simple. If that is okay with you, Jacob. Maybe a few people in the backyard."

"I love that idea." Jacob was not a fan of large gatherings to begin with.

"Sooner than later?" She looked at him with a smirk.

"Like how soon are we talking. We can get married today!"

"Not that soon. We have to get the marriage license and the minister. Figure out some little details."

"She is right, Jacob. Next week is better," Deanna broke her silence. Everyone turned and looked at her. "Once you're married, you can work on a brother or sister for me."

"Deanna!" MaryAnn shouted, her cheeks turning slightly pink.

"What? I mean, it would be nice."

Everyone started to chuckle.

"Girl has a point," Mark spoke up.

"Okay, okay, guys, let us all not all jump on this train. I would like to take it a day at a time." Mary looked at Jacob. "Can we talk in private?"

"Yes. Everything okay?" Jacob grew instantly worried.

"Yes. Come with me." She took his hand and guided him to the back bedroom while everyone else went into the kitchen.

"What's wrong?"

"Nothing, my love. I just needed a minute alone with my fiancé to soak everything in." She wrapped her arms around his waist and placed her head on his shoulder.

"What else is bothering you?"

"It's just a wave of emotions catching up, that is all. How soon do you want to get married?"

"Whenever you're ready. If you want to do it today, then let's. If you want to do it next week, I am okay with that. If you want to wait and do it next year, I am okay with that too."

"What about kids? We never talked about that. Do you want any?"

"I have one who is awesome, and if she will let me, I would like to adopt her once we are married. If you want more, then I am okay with that too. If you do not, that is fine. I just want to spend the rest of my life with you, no matter what, making you happy."

"Jacob." She took a deep breath. "I love you."

"I love you too, Mary. Always have and always will."

She looked up with her glistening eyes into his, staring into each other's eyes for what seemed like eternity.

"Mary, are you sure you do not want the bells and whistle of a wedding? Full uniform, in the church? Big reception?"

"Nope. I just want it to be you and I with our daughter and a few friends. Something little. A little cake for us, cupcakes for everyone else. Have a cookout-style wedding."

"I love the idea."

"I want to ask Mark to give me away. Do you think he will?"

"Mary, there is no doubt in my mind that he will."

"Do you think next Saturday is too soon for us to put this together?"

"No, I think with the help of Stacy, you two can manage to pull it off. I can get Mark to schedule me off the day before and the week after. Can you reschedule your clients?"

"Since I went back last year, I have been more focused on the business. I have some loyal clients whom I still do, but I really am not on the floor too much, especially with the expansion and all the additives we are adding on."

"So you're open."

"Yes, I am open. What do you have in mind?"

"Escaping, us two, on a honeymoon. We can see if Mark and Stacy will allow us to use their beach house and just going for the week. Deanna can most likely stay with them. What do you think?"

"I have never been to the beach. I would love it."

They heard a light tap on the door. Jacob opened the door to see Deanna standing there.

"You don't have to have a baby. I am sorry if that upset you." Her face dropped to the ground. She felt her mother was upset because of her words.

"Oh, Dee. Baby girl, no, I am not upset with you. I love your excitement over it. I just needed to talk with Jacob and take in this very moment. So much commotion. I just needed to breathe."

"So you are okay?"

"More than okay." MaryAnn looked at Jacob. "Jacob and I, decided, if Stacy can help me pull this off, next Saturday we will be getting married. Jacob is calling the realtor and putting his house on the market today, and if he wants, he can move in here."

"Now? Today?"

"Yes."

"Are you sure?"

"Jacob, I am very sure. You just have to behave until, ya know, the wedding night." MaryAnn giggled at Deanna making a disgusted face.

"GROSS, MOM!" Deanna walked out of the room. Jacob and MaryAnn filled the air with pure laughter.

"Now that, babe, was epic. Mary, you are full of surprises today."

"So what do you think?"

"I say yes. I want to live with you." He leaned over and gently placed a kiss onto her lips. "But right now, I am starving, and Stacy must have warmed up the bacon."

"Well, that will teach you, next time we eat first before you pop some questions." Teasing Jacob, MaryAnn darted out of the room.

Chasing her to the living room, he met up to her, started to tickle her sides. Laughter filled the room.

"Oh really?"

"Jacob, truce." Catching her breath, he finally let her up.

"Okay, you two, get a room," biting into a piece of bacon, Mark shouted.

"Oh, they have one, but Jacob has to be good according to Mom!" Deanna yelled out, pretending to gag.

"Jacob is moving in. Stacy, do you think you can help me plan the wedding?"

"Sure. Do we have a date set?"

"Yes, next week."

"Well then. We have some work cut out for us."

"I just want it quite simple. Cookout style. Sundress. Deanna to stand up with me."

"Mark, Mary and I have two big things to ask you."

"It's yes to both."

"You do not even know what we are going to ask."

"Mary, whatever it is, the answer is yes."

"Well, Jacob, I guess we get both of his kidneys and…"

Once again, the room broke out into laughter.

"In all seriousness, Mark, will you give me away?"

"Yes, Mary, I would be honored."

"And once you are done giving her away, will you be my best man?"

"Well, Jacob. I will be already up there. I might as well stand next to ya."

"Whoa, you are honored to give Mary up there and it's just a convenience that you will already be up there?"

"Calm yourself, of course I am honored you asked for me to stand with you." Mark gave Jacob a shove, only to embrace him in a hug. "Both of your parents and grandparents would be darn proud of you too."

"Stacy, let's leave these two girls to their hug. We can go have breakfast and start writing down some ideas." MaryAnn giggled as she swiftly walked to the kitchen.

"I can't with her." Jacob shook his head.

"Well, now you're stuck with her."

"Nah, Mark, I am not stuck. I am lucky."

"You sure are."

They all sat around the breakfast table, talking about the wedding, sharing one another's ideas, coming up with different solutions to possible issues that may come up. Jacob came up with the idea of hiring Joel, Moe's Pizza shop, to cater the wedding, cookout style. MaryAnn was very admitted that she wanted more like a cookout, finger foods.

"So while we are all sitting here, talking wedding, I have something to ask." Jacob winked at Mary. "Deanna, I was wondering, after your mom and I get married, what do you think about me adopting you?"

"Are you kidding me? That is freaking awesome. I love that idea!" Deanna jumped up from her seat and ran to Jacob, bear-hugging him, almost knocking him out of his seat.

"Well, that sums it all up." MaryAnn smiled. "Jacob, why don't you call the realtor? I am going to call the salon, Joel, and the church. Monday we will have to apply for the marriage license."

"And once you do that, let me know. I will have her put a little pep in her step, if you know what I mean."

"Thanks, Mark."

"I will handle the florist and I think you, Dee, and I need to head out in a few to start looking for the dress."

"I will be very impressed if you two pull this off in a week."

"Oh, not only will we pull it off in time, my dear." Stacy got up from her seat. "But we will have a whole day to spare and rehearse."

"Oh, is that so?" Mark smirked at his wife.

"It is. Mary, we shall get moving. These guys can get the kitchen cleaned up."

"Um."

"Go, Mary, I got this." Jacob picked her hand up and kissed it. "Go find your dress. Talk to Joel and the pastor."

"Are you sure?"

"Yes, my love. Now go." He looked over at Deanna. "You too, go. Have fun. Help your mom pick out the perfect sundress."

"Okay." Deanna paused for a moment. "Okay... Dad."

Jacob loved hearing her say that. He knows Eli will forever be her father, but he will be her angel father now while he will have the chance to raise her into a fine young lady, such as her mother, teach her how a guy truly treats a woman.

MaryAnn's eyes moistened. Hearing Deanna call Jacob Dad just set everything into place. Standing up, she grabbed her plate, trying to hide her emotions.

"Dee, thank you. I love hearing you call me Dad."

"Well, next week will be official. You will be my dad. Then hopefully soon after that, I will share the same last name as you and Mommy."

MaryAnn turned around, her eyes wide.

"Deanna, you want to change your last name?"

"Yes."

"Are you sure?"

"Yes, Mom, I am very sure. When my father was alive, he lived two lives, he was not faithful to you, nor was he to me. He hurt you, and in return hurt me. Jacob, he has always been there for you and me, Mom. Even when we did not know the truth, he was there. He has not missed a single birthday of mine or Christmas. He has always been there. Now fast forward, fourteen years later, he is still here and marrying you. He has always been my dad. I just never saw it. I did not know I needed to see it. In order to move on from the past, you have to start fresh. So you change your last name and so do I." Deanna grabbed her plate, stood up, and walked to the sink. Placing the plate into the sink, she turned, and everyone was still in silence, shock, staring at her.

Jacob could not believe what he heard. She was right; he has not missed a single birthday or holiday when it came to Deanna or MaryAnn. He could not believe she remembered that. Getting up from the table, he walked over to her and embraced her into a tight hug.

"Dad, I can't breathe. You're squeezing me so tight," Deanna joked, trying to break the serious tone in the air.

"Oh, sorry kid." He released her, kissed her on her forehead.

"Just kidding." Giggling, she returned his hug.

"Well, now you got everyone in tears, let's get moving." Stacy grabbed her purse and MaryAnn's hand.

"Okay, okay. Come on, Dee." Mary smiled, kissed Jacob, and headed out the door.

They drove into town. First stop was the church. MaryAnn walked up to the office door. Thankfully the pastor was in. She tapped on the door.

"MaryAnn. What a delightful pleasure to see you today."

"Hello, Pastor Green."

"What can I do for you today?"

MaryAnn lifted her hand, showing him the ring.

"Jacob asked me to marry him this morning."

"Oh, my word, praise the Lord. He finally did it and you said yes. So when is the big day?"

"That is why I am here. We want to get married, in our yard, next Saturday, and it would mean the world to the both of us if you were able to do it on such short notice."

"Well, that's fast. Let me look at my calendar to make sure I do not have any other commitments that day." He walked over to his desk and pulled out his planner. "Nope, I am actually clear all day. What time are you thinking?"

"We are doing a cookout backyard wedding, so ceremony at one. Does that work for you?"

"It sure does. Now usually I have my newlyweds come to a few classes before the big day, but for you two, I know this is a forever commitment and I know you both have the Lord as your Savior. If it is okay with you, I will put this together as I see to fit."

"Fine with me. I would like that."

"Now, are you two making your own vows?"

"You know, we did not discuss that, but I am going to say yes."

"Good. That is all I need to know."

"Thank you so much, Pastor Green! This means the world to me. It is going to be a small ceremony. A few of our closest friends. So make sure your wife is there too."

"That is genuinely nice of you. I will make sure."

"Pastor Green, what will be the fee be for you to perform the ceremony?"

"What fee? Just consider it a wedding gift."

"No, I can't do that."

"Yes, MaryAnn, you can and you will. Now, go. Let me start your ceremony paperwork."

"Thank you, Pastor Green." MaryAnn gave him a hug before turning around and heading out the office.

"So is he able?" Stacy asked as MaryAnn opened the door.

"Yes, and he refused my payment offer."

"I figured he would." Stacy smiled as she pulled out of the parking lot. "Next Joel's, then to find your dress and your dress as well, Deanna."

"Yours too, Stacy. I would love if you would stand up there with Deanna and I."

"Really?"

"Yes! Would you?"

"I would be truly honored"

"Then it's settled."

Joel's pizza place was only a few blocks from the church. This time they all were coming in.

"I wonder if sweet Taylor will be seating us today," MaryAnn sarcastically spoke.

"Sweet Taylor?"

"Stacy, she is the girl that was making moves on Dad last year in front of Mom."

"Oh." Stacy shook her head as she opened the door.

As they walked through the doors, Deanna giggled. There stood waiting to seat them was Taylor. By the look of her face, she remembered MaryAnn.

"Hello, Taylor." MaryAnn smirked as she put her left hand, ring shining, on the counter. "Haven't seen you here lately. Can I have a corner booth seat for us three ladies, please?"

Looking down, she noticed the ring.

"Hello, MaryAnn. I had left town for a little bit. Let me show you to your booth." Taking them to the back-corner booth, Taylor sat them, gave them the menus, and walked away.

"Mary, I have never seen this side of you." With shock tone, Stacy just looked at MaryAnn.

"She just rubs me the wrong way." Shrugging her shoulders, she looked at the menu.

"MaryAnn, Deanna, and Stacy, what do I have the pleasure to get you to drink?"

"Scared your waitress off again, did I?" A slight giggle came from the menu.

"Ugh, yes. You keep doing that, I am going to have to hire you to work here."

"Speaking of hiring, do you have a moment?"

"Sure, let me grab a chair. Taylor,"—Joel motioned Taylor back to the table—"drinks, can you get them please?"

"Yes, sir. What would everyone like?"

"I will have an unsweetened tea please. Deanna will have a water with lemon."

"Make that two waters with lemon, my dear." Stacy gave her an apologetic tone.

"Grab me a raspberry tea please."

"Yes, sir. I will be right back." Taylor moved swiftly to begin to fill their drinks.

"What's up, Mary?"

"Do you cater?"

"Depends on the size, but I have."

"What about finger foods, cookout, for under, let's say, twenty people?"

"That is doable. So fries, onion rings, burgers, or cheeseburgers. Side salads? Something like that?"

"Yes, just like that. Any way you can pull it off for next Saturday around one thirty?"

"I do not see why not. Are you having a party, Deanna?"

"Actually,"—MaryAnn pulled out her hand from under the table—"Jacob asked me to marry him and I said yes."

All of a sudden, they heard a crash. Taylor dropped the tray of drinks, hearing the news.

"Oh, I am so sorry, Joel. There is a lip in the carpet, and I caught it." Her voice was shaky.

"It's okay, Taylor, just clean it up and get the drinks."

She bent down and started to pick up the cups and ice, hearing the conversation continue.

"So as I was saying, I said yes, and we set the date for Saturday. We are only asking our closest friends. We want to keep it small. He is putting his house on the market today and moving in tonight. Once we get married, he asked to file the paperwork to adopt Deanna, which she excitedly agreed to and decided to change her last name too. We would love if you and your family could be there and if your shop could cater."

"Out of all the other places, you are asking me?"

"Yes. It was here last year that Jacob and I connected on another level. You have been there through everything, offering to help in any way, food, donations, anything. You are the only person we would ask."

"Mary, this means a lot. You can count us in. We would not miss it for the world."

"Good." MaryAnn smiled as she looked over at Stacy. "This is coming together better than I thought it would."

"Joel, I will be paying for it."

"No, Stacy. I can—"

"Nonsense, Mary, I want to."

"Well, it will be hard to pay when I refuse to give you a price."

"Joel, we need to cover the food at least."

"Nope. You can return by being nicer to my waitress." He smirked.

"Well, I think she needs to put out that little crush she has on my future husband. It is pretty obvious. She did drop the tray when she heard the news."

"I will have a talk with her about it." Joel shook his head. "Feels like I am the principal in high school."

"Your drinks." Taylor walked up with a new tray.

"Taylor, will there be an issue if I asked you to work the cater job I was just hired for? Jacob and MaryAnn's wedding?"

"No, no, sir."

"Okay. Just making sure. Bring the Nonna pie that just came out over please."

"Yes, sir."

"How's that, Mary?" he asked, chuckling at the faces of all three ladies sitting at the table.

"Well, okay then."

"Put the menus down. I just made fresh Nonna pie. You will all love it."

They sat there, talking, going over the food options, ideas, as they devoured the Nonna pie. They decided on sliders, cheeseburger, hamburger, bacon cheeseburgers, fries, and onion rings. He is even going to have one of his guys take care of the grill so the sliders are fresh and offered hot dogs as well. Corn on the cob will be provided as well and homemade potato and macaroni salad.

"What about your cucumber and onion salad?"

"Is that a special request, Dee?"

"It sure is. It's the best!"

"Well, it will be there. So the ceremony is at one. I will be there by eleven to start setting up and prepping, getting my people in order. I will shut down the shop for the day, just for you, and I do not want to hear anything about cost or money. Money is not everything in life. Besides, you gave my brother-in-law the dealership back."

"What? Wait, Charlie is your brother-in-law?"

"He is my wife's brother."

"That makes Eli your nephew."

"It does." He put his head down. "I am sorry I never told you, Mary."

"No, it's really okay. Things are starting to make sense on why everyone has been willing to help me."

"No, no. It has nothing to do with Eli. It all stems from your parents. Your parents were such loving, caring people. They taught many of us that helping someone before yourself is the right thing. It is something that has stuck with many of us and who better to help but their daughter who is just a sweet as they were?"

"Is there any other of Eli's family in town?"

"Nope, you found the last of me, that I know about. His family was different."

"They sure were." She took a deep breath and shook her head. She will not let that man step into her new life at any given point. "Joel, do you think Linda would make my cake?"

"Oh, I am sure she would be honored. She should be at the bakery."

"Perfect. We will head there next," Stacy perked up. "I say let us use the bathroom and hit the road. I am excited to dress shop!"

"I agree." MaryAnn and Deanna got up. "Joel, thank you for everything!" She gave him a big hug.

"You are so welcome!" Joel started to gather the dishes from the table.

Waving goodbye, they left the pizza shop, only to walk six doors down to the bakery. Walking into the door, the bell dinged.

"I'll be right out," Linda shouted from the back. Taking the cookies from the oven, she placed the pan on the counter. "How can I help—oh hey, MaryAnn!" She ran from behind the counter. "Congratulations!"

"Wow, news travel fast."

"Well, it is on the front page of the *Community Times*."

"What? Wait, what is?"

"That your expansion will be complete soon."

"Oh, I totally forgot about that article." She chuckled.

"What do you think I was complimenting you on?"

MaryAnn picked her hand up.

"Jacob and I, we are getting married."

Linda shrieked with pure excitement along with saying words in pure Italian.

"Um, Linda, what was that?" Deanna could not help but laugh.

"Oh, dear child, I am so sorry. When I get so excited my Italian spits out."

"So we just left Joel. He agreed to cater for me, and I was wondering—"

"Yes, I got your cake."

"Okay, I want a small cake for Jacob and I and cupcakes for the guests."

"Now that is perfect. I love that idea. I will also make some pastries to go with it."

"We are doing a cookout backyard wedding, like twenty or less. So it is basically finger foods."

"Good. I will take care of the snacks."

"So your brochure here says one tier starts at—"

"Oh shoot, those are old. Let me just take them. The prices have changed." Linda quickly grabbed all the brochures.

"Oh, okay, so what is the cost of the cupcakes, one tier, and snacks?"

"I am not sure." Linda smirked.

"Do not pull a Joel."

"Husband and wife think alike."

"Linda."

"MaryAnn." She smiled. "Deanna, tell her, family helps family." Linda winked.

"Yeah, Mom. Family helps family."

MaryAnn could not hold back the emotions any longer. Her eyes filled up with tears; one blink and they were overflowing down her cheeks.

"I will never understand why he chose to leave the details of his aunts and uncles out. We would have loved to have been part of your lives, you and Joel, Charlie and Dawn."

"We will never know. But you know now, and although it was only by marriage for you and blood for you, you are family no matter what. His father would be so disappointed with him."

"Thank you."

Stacy, Deanna, and Linda group-hugged MaryAnn. So much emotion. Learning people you knew your whole life were actually family and they could not tell you and, when they could, did not know how to tell you since you have been through so much already.

"You leave the goodies up to me. Where are you ladies heading off to next?"

"Well, we are going dress shopping. Then to the craft store to get everything we will need. The boys tend to have challenged us, so I will exceed that challenge." Stacy smiled.

"Well, go, ladies, go have fun. Oh, hey, Mary, did you think of a DJ?"

"You know, Linda, that slipped my mind. I didn't even think of that since we are keeping it small."

"Call Charlie. Matthew does DJ on the side."

"Oh really? If we can find our dresses by three, we can stop there. The dealership is open until five."

"Perfect. It's one now, get going!" Linda pushed them out the door, only to pick up the phone and call Charlie to give the details on what was going on.

The afternoon was filled with dress after dress, decisions after decisions, stopping the car dealership to be told they were not going to pay for Matthew's DJ service. MaryAnn just could not believe how well this was all coming together and how generous everyone was being. It was close to seven when they pulled back into the driveway. Jacob came out the door with Mark.

"Don't just stand there looking all cute. Help us unload please," Stacy shouted.

"Send you out in the morning and you return home after dinner. What the heck were you doing?" Mark shook his head as he joked.

"Let's see, we booked the pastor, baker, cater, DJ, embarrassed a waitress." Hearing that, Jacob spit out his water and looked at MaryAnn who just shrugged her shoulders as Stacy continued, "Got our dresses, shoes, and all the decorations, paper products that will be needed."

"Um, so go back to the embarrassing waitress part." Jacob looked at MaryAnn.

"Is that the only thing you heard? Not the fact that the only thing left for the wedding is to decorate and make things, oh, and the guest list and to let them know?" MaryAnn looked right back at him.

"Oh, I heard all that, but I am curious about the waitress."

"Mom did not mean to. She was bringing a tray of drinks and overheard Mom telling Joel about you two getting married, and the girl dropped the tray of drinks. You know, the girl who was flirting with you last year, Dad."

"You made that girl leave town for a while."

"Nope, she left on her own, but what Joel did would make anyone crawl back in their shell."

"What did he do?"

"Blatantly asked if she would be okay to cater next Saturday or would she have issues."

Jacob just started to laugh. "I wasn't even there and you're making girls cry."

He opened the back of the truck. "Did you buy the whole craft store?" he asked, seeing the loads of bags.

"We left a few items." Stacy glared at Mark as he rolled his eyes.

"Just four carts' worth." Deanna chuckled. She was enjoying this moment just as much as the adults were.

"That's it. Heck, amateurs." Jacob smirked as he grabbed as many bags as he could.

They brought all the bags into the house. MaryAnn organized them by category for the big day.

"What do you think of this, Jacob, to put on the tables? Oh, and by the way, Pastor Green called and said they are bringing tables and chairs from the church."

"That's awesome. Honestly I did not even think about that."

"I know. Neither did I."

"It's coming together, my love. I called and my house is officially listed. The realtor seems to think it will go fast."

"That is awesome, Jacob."

Jacob and Mark carried some of the bags to the back spare room while Stacy and Deanna started to craft things. MaryAnn just stood there, taking it all in. A soft knock on her front door pulled her from her thoughts. Everyone stopped, looked at the door. MaryAnn walked over, opened the door, and just stood there. In disbelief, she did not understand. Jacob sensed something was not right and quickly walked to his fiancée's side.

"Tabby, what are you doing here?" Jacob broke the silence.

"I wanted to talk to MaryAnn," Tabby said, standing there, looking lost, scared, with a baby in her arms. Eli's baby.

"Come in." MaryAnn finally found her voice. "We can talk in private out in the sunroom." She looked at Jacob. "I will be fine. Go make a spot in the closet for your clothes. Take Dee with you, please."

"Okay." Jacob understood the hint.

"Mary, what do you think of this?" Stacy asked as they walked through the kitchen. "I figure just simple."

"Stacy, it's actually perfect. If you need me, just knock. I will be in the sunroom. Tabby wants to talk."

"Just remember Luke 6:37: 'Judge not, and you will not be judged; condemn not, and you will not be condemned; forgive, and you will be forgiven.'"

"Thank you." MaryAnn opened the sunroom door. She motioned for Tabby to go in ahead of her so she could close the door back over.

"I am sorry to come to your home."

"It is okay." She took a deep breath. "She is beautiful, reminds me of Dee when she was that little."

"Thank you. I named her Hope Elizabeth Baker."

Hearing the last name hit MaryAnn just a little harder than she thought it would. Taking a deep breath, she remembered the verse that Stacy just recited.

"Love it. What can I do for you?"

"I wanted to know, well…" Tabby had trouble getting her words out. "I put the house on the market, and it has sold. I go for closing in two days. I am moving back home, where I have family, where I am accepted and no longer looked at as the home-wrecker."

Sadness filled over MaryAnn. She knew Tabby loved the house and it was the one connection besides the baby she had with Eli.

"I am sorry my niece fought with your daughter last year. My sister pulled her from the school and moved back home too."

"I am sorry you felt you had to move to be happy. I never wanted that for you."

"I know. You're just so well loved in this town. Even Eli's family does not want a single thing to do with Hope or I."

"One day, they will. You just have to give it time."

"I hope. I just wanted to let you know that and I wanted to ask that, maybe your daughter can meet her half sister?"

"I will bring her in, but you have to let me talk to her first. Also understand they will not be sharing the same last name much longer once Jacob adopts her after the wedding."

"Congratulations. At least one of us can have a happy ending."

"Tabby, you can too. You have to let Eli go. Holding on to him will only deepen the depression you are in. Once I let him go, my world started to rebuild."

"Thank you. Maybe one day."

"Okay, just hang tight right here. Let me go talk to her first." MaryAnn stood up and left the room.

"Everything okay?"

"Yes, Mark. I need to go talk to Deanna."

"You are doing the right thing, kiddo," Mark whispered as she walked by.

MaryAnn walked to her bedroom door. Hearing Deanna laugh at Jacob, the warm feeling in the air, she knew she was truly doing the right thing. Deanna deserved to know her sister.

"Hey."

"You okay?"

"I am, Jacob. I need to talk to Deanna and as her dad, I want you to stay."

"Okay."

"Deanna, my girl, I need to give you an option, but first you need to know some details. That woman, Tabby, is the mistress of your father. The baby she is holding, her name is Hope Elizabeth Baker."

Deanna's eyes grew. Baker. She was starting to put pieces together.

"Yes. The baby is your half sister. It is your choice. Do you want to meet her? Or do you prefer not to? Tabby is moving away, about two hours away, and wanted you to have this chance."

"It's not the baby's fault that our dad was a horrible person," Deanna whispered. "Yes. I think it would be the right thing to do. I have a little sister. But this does not mean that I do not want another one, you know."

"You, my child, you're a brave girl but one with great character. Never change that." MaryAnn pulled Deanna into her arms. "Jacob, you come too, please. You are Deanna's dad and my husband—well, almost. This is a family moment."

"Okay." He took Mary's hand.

They all walked down the hall and into the kitchen. No words were exchanged. MaryAnn opened the door and entered first, followed by Jacob and finally, Deanna.

"Deanna, this is Tabby."

"Hello."

"Hello, Deanna. Please forgive me."

"It wasn't just you."

"I know."

"I will forgive you."

"Thank you. Deanna, this is Hope Elizabeth, your little sister."

Hope looked up, reached her hands out, and smiled at Deanna. Without hesitation, Deanna put her hands out and took Hope. They sat down on the floor and just played. The baby giggled as Deanna laughed. Tabby watched the two of them interacted. Could not help herself, she began to cry.

"You two are always welcome in our home." MaryAnn reached out to Tabby and wrapped her arms around her in a hug. Jacob, Stacy, and Mark just stood there. "You are forgiven."

CHAPTER 11

The Wedding

The day had come. MaryAnn and Stacy spent the whole week making the backdrop, putting together things for the tables, finalizing the song choice, contacting the guests that were to be invited, making sure the backyard was ready. Jacob and Mark helped where they could, but between moving Jacob's things out of his home and work, their time was tied up.

"Jacob, your wife, she has a heart of gold." Pastor Green shook Jacob's hand.

"That she does." Jacob smiled. He was standing in Deanna's room, looking in the mirror, making sure his shirt was done exactly right.

"She shocked the whole town, suggesting for Tabby to stay in town, by your house instead. The Lord works through that girl more than we will ever know."

"That is why I love her more and more every single day. What really took that shock to the next level was when she invited her to the wedding."

"She is a true child of Christ." Pastor Green smiled. "Well, I just came to tell you it is time."

"Finally," Jacob joked. He followed the pastor down the hall, out the front door, and into the backyard, down between the set of chairs. Pastor Green stood in the middle as Jacob stood next to him at the makeshift altar. Looking out, he saw their close friends, from the station to the salon. The sun was shining through the trees. The birds were chirping, making this moment the most perfect moment.

The music started to play. Stacy was the first to appear from the sunroom wearing a pretty pale-yellow sundress and flip-flops, carrying a trio of tiger lilies. Jacob chuckled when he noticed the flip-flops. Mary was not kidding about a cookout wedding. Stacy reached the pastor and smiled over at Jacob as she took her spot. Deanna made her way out the sunroom wearing an off-white version sundress along with her flip-flops, holding on to a trio of white lilies. She slowly made her way to the altar where she hugged Jacob before taking her place next to Stacy. The music lowered. Everyone stood, making it harder for Jacob to see. The music began to play. Butterflies appeared in Jacob's stomach. Everyone turned to look for the bride.

"You ready, kiddo? This is your moment."

"I am." MaryAnn looked up at Mark, smiling from ear to ear. "I have been ready."

"Let's do this thing." He stepped out the side door of the sunroom, walked down the steps, then reached for her hand to help guide her down.

Locking their arms together, they began the walk behind everyone until they reached the opening between the chairs. Pausing just for a moment, MaryAnn locked on Jacob's eyes. She smiled, and at that moment, that was the only person she saw. Nobody else was there; it was just them two.

Jacob watched. He saw the door open but still could not see his bride. Then a moment later, she was there, wearing a beautiful off-white figure-fitting gown. Hugging her hips was just a small train, but her veil dragged past her train. She was holding a combination of the tiger lily and white lily. No wonder why she insisted that he was to wear his dress uniform. Jacob could not hold back his emotions as the tears filled his eyes and ran down his cheeks. She walked with elegance. To him, Mark was not there; it was just Mary. Taking a deep breath, he wiped his tears away.

"Good afternoon to all. Let us bow our heads in prayer," Pastor Green began to speak as the music lowered with Mary's arrival. "Dear heavenly Father, we come to you on this beautiful glorious day, to join MaryAnn's and Jacob's hand in marriage, to finally, Lord, bring their lives together as one. We ask that you bless them in their years to come with great joy and tremendous happiness, for it is only because of you, Lord, that we are here today. Amen. Who gives this bride to this groom?"

Without hesitation, all the men in the audience stood and replied along with Mark.

"WE DO!"

MaryAnn turned around to see them all standing. She could not hold back; her eyes overflowed. She could not believe they all stood up.

"Well, they all do." Pastor Green smirked. "Jacob, you may take your bride's hand." Pastor Green took the rings from Mark. "These rings are a symbol of hope, of everlasting life, a bond which shall not be broken. Jacob, place this ring on to her left ring finger and repeat after me."

"I, Jacob, take you, Mary, to be my wife, to have and to hold until death do us part."

"I, Jacob, take you, Mary, to be my wife, to have and to hold until death do us part."

"MaryAnn, take this ring and place it on Jacob's left ring finger and repeat after me. I, Mary, take you, Jacob, to be my husband, to have and to hold until death do us part."

"I, Mary, take you, Jacob, to be my husband, to have and to hold until death do us part."

"A marriage should not be taken lightly. A marriage should be filled with love, understanding, crazy times, fun times. Honestly, when I was asked to marry these two, I thought to myself, well it is about time, then I was asked to marry them in a week and I said to myself, 'Wow. Okay.' In reality, this relationship, this marriage, this love, is one to compare and look up to. What these two have done is beat the odds, have returned to each other, and there is one reason that we are here today. Their faith in the Lord brought them to this moment. A moment of love. Ecclesiastes 4:9 says, 'Two are better than one, because they have a good return for their labor: If either of them falls down, one can help the other up. But pity anyone who falls and has no one to help them up. Also, if two lie down together, they will keep warm. But how can one keep warm alone?' 'Love is patient, love is kind. It does not envy, it does not boast, it is not proud. It does not dishonor others, it is not self-seeking, it is not easily angered, it keeps no record of wrongs. Love does not delight in evil but rejoices with the truth. It always protects, always trusts, always hopes, always perseveres. Love never fails. But where there are prophecies, they will cease; where there are tongues, they will be stilled; where there is knowledge, it will pass away' [1 Corinthians 13:4–8]. These are verses to remember as times goes on and a tough day arrives. At this time, MaryAnn will say her vows."

"Jacob, you are my light to my darkness. You make me want to smile even when I am crying. Through all the tragic events that life has given me, you have stood there to pick me up with each and every step. You wiped the tears off my checks. You waited, and I am so glad you did. You make life worth each breath I take. You complete me in every sense. I love you, now and forevermore."

Pastor Green nodded his head for Jacob to say his.

"MaryAnn, my Mary, I knew from the time you dropped that book in the hall in school that we were meant to be. If I had to wait a thousand years I would have. You are worth every single bit of the wait. My life is not complete unless you are in it. You and Deanna. You are my family. Nothing can rip us apart. I love you beyond the stars and past the moon. I cannot wait for tomorrow to begin because I know it begins with you in it."

"Mary and Jacob chose not to do a unity candle or any other type of gesture. They have something special instead to do." Pastor Green handed Mary the package.

"Deanna, there was nothing more unifying us as a family, then this." She handed the package to Dee. Deanna opened it, read the first page, and looked at Jacob and back at her mother.

"They are her adoption papers. All that is left is the judge's signature to make her an official Shaffer," Jacob announced.

"And I am here to do that." Judge Williams stood up, walked up to them, took his pen out, and signed the papers. "No questions asked. I know what this means to all three of you, especially to you, Deanna."

Deanna, full of emotions, hugged Jacob tightly, along with Mary. There was not one dried eye around. The judged returned to his seat as Deanna returned to her spot.

"Well, not that we can top that off, I just have one thing left to do." Pastor Green looked at Jacob. "Jacob, you may now FINALLY kiss your bride. I pronounce you husband and wife."

"Oh, with great pleasure," Jacob spoke as he gently took both his hands on each side of MaryAnn's face. Leaning in, his lips met hers. She wrapped her arms around his waist, bringing him closer to her. "Now, I no longer have to behave myself, Mrs. Shaffer," he whispered in her ear, as the crowd erupted in cheer. Her cheeks began to glow a bright blush, hoping nobody else heard him.

"It is with great pleasure and honor to introduce the new Mr. and Mrs. Jacob Shaffer."

The trumpets sounded as Jacob scooped MaryAnn up into his arms and carried her down the aisle. Deanna followed behind them, along with Mark and Stacy, as everyone applauded and cheered.

"Where are we going?" MaryAnn was confused. They had to set the tables up so everyone could enjoy food and drinks as well as dancing.

"In the limo, my love. We need our pictures taken. Charles hired a photographer for us."

"But we have to set up the tables."

"Already taken care of. Surprise!" Mark hugged MaryAnn.

"You guys! Thank you." MaryAnn climbed into the limo; Deanna was already claiming her seat. "Come on, Mark and Stacy, you're part of this family too."

"We are honored."

They drove down to a beautiful spot by the lake, taking picture after picture: Deanna, with both of her parents, just the bride, the bride and the groom, and the list went on. The day was perfect in every aspect, from the weather to the birds.

"I am ready to return to the party. My husband owes me a dance."

"I love the sound of that, 'husband.' I love you, my wife."

"Ugh, you guys are gagging me." Deanna pretended to be sick.

"Oh really!" Jacob looked over at her. "Then let me gag you some more." He kissed his wife yet again and again.

"Okay, you two need to get a room!" Mark and Stacy shouted at the exact same time.

"Oh, we have one already and I do not have to be good any-more," Jacob joked, making Deanna gag even more. The limo came to a stop. The driver opened the door as laughter funneled out. Jacob reached his hand out to Mary. "Come, my wife, I owe you a dance."

"Yes, my husband, you do."

They walked hand in hand back to the back yard, only to stop. They could not believe they were in the same backyard. Tables on each side of a dance floor, a floor they did not order, yet it was there. Lights hanging in the trees with floating lanterns, something else extra. Joel's crew was busy cooking up burgers; Linda's crew was busy catering to the snacks. The cookout wedding had a fancy backyard reception and it was absolutely breathtaking. The DJ noticed the bride and groom and rang out the bells over his equipment.

"Everyone, let's welcome back the beautiful bride, Mrs. MaryAnn Shaffer, her husband, Mr. Jacob Shaffer, and their daugh-ter, Deanna Shaffer!" the DJ spoke over the microphone. "Would the bride and groom make their way to the middle of the dance floor for the first dance?"

Jacob took Mary's hand and led her to the middle of the floor. A sweet romantic song began to play. His right hand laid on her back while his left hand held on to her hand. He stared into her blue eyes, placing a slight kiss on her nose. He finally got his forever moment.

"If I could freeze one moment, it would be this one. You look beautiful. I cannot believe you are my wife. I am the luckiest guy alive."

"You're just saying that because I am your wife."

"Sure, but I am saying it because it is true. Every ounce."

"Well, I am the luckiest girl alive. I married my best friend, finally. My book of life may have started out bumpy. It wasn't the best first half of a book for sure, but now, with you, this chapter, I am saying is the beginning of a new book of my life filled with a happy ending. You are my happily ever after, Jacob Shaffer. I love you."

"I love you, MaryAnn Shaffer, forever and always."

The end.

Take delight in the Lord,
and he will give you the desires of your heart.
—Psalm 37

ABOUT THE AUTHOR

Maranda Ballard is a wife and mother to one amazing little girl and a stepmother to one cool dude. A cosmetologist in the southern part of New Jersey, she enjoys writing. Writing helps Maranda to escape from everyday life. She enjoys sitting on the porch or at the campsite, coming up with ideas for an adventure in the book. Enjoying time with her husband and her children gives her all the inspiration she needs to create a romance filled with love and challenges. With the support of her family and her older sister, Maranda's dreams came true with this book, her first to be published. Maranda would tell anyone who would listen, "Dreams can come true if you work hard enough."

CPSIA information can be obtained
at www.ICGtesting.com
Printed in the USA
BVHW071128230421
605721BV00004B/457